Copyright

The unauthorized reproduction or distribution of a copyrighted work is illegal. Criminal copyright infringement, including infringement without monetary gain, is investigated by the FBI and is punishable by fines and federal imprisonment.

Please purchase only authorized editions and do not participate in or encourage, the piracy of copyrighted material. Your support of author's rights is appreciated.

This book is a work of fiction. Names, characters, places and incidents are the products of the author's imagination or used fictitiously. Any resemblance to actual events, locales or persons, living or dead is entirely coincidental.

Wicked Predator copyrighted 2022 by Delta James and Felicity Brandon

---

Cover Design: Dar Albert of Wicked Smart Designs

Editing: Sandy Ebel of Personal Touch Editing

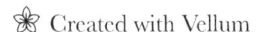

❦ Created with Vellum

WICKED PREDATOR

FELICITY BRANDON AND DELTA JAMES

*This Book is Dedicated to Our
Families and Our Readers
Without You, None of This Would be Possible.*

*What Started as a Lark Between Two
Shark Week Nerds Has Now
Become a Series*

PROLOGUE

Their primary mission a failure, five brave men sacrificed themselves to scuttle the USS Kraken, vowing to protect the sub, its secrets, and their failure from ever being known. Each man damned himself and the sons that would follow to a life on eternal patrol as masters of the deep.

CHAPTER 1

Logan

Slicing through the water, the Shortfin Mako Shark darted just beneath the waves as if he was playing with the surf. The shark swam with such glee that anyone watching would have sworn his playful leaps were impossible, but this was no ordinary shark. This was Logan Knight. Propelling through the ocean, he swam on for miles before something insidious captured his attention.

Pausing at the surface, the shark halted—just stopped in the water—poking its snout above the spray. If it was possible, his eyes widened, heart racing as he surveyed the state of the sea. Beyond him, for hundreds of feet, crude black oil crept over the surface, spreading farther by the moment, the accelerating wind and relentless current aiding its escape.

He bobbed in the water, shaking his head as

though he couldn't believe his eyes, and then, just as the dark slick crawled toward him, he turned, diving down away from the horror of the pollution. He journeyed for miles, fueled by the fury swirling in his head.

Who could have done this? How dare they poison the beautiful ecosystem?

By the time he neared his destination, he was ready for blood. Logan rose to the surface, eyeing the enormous yacht, *Top Secret*, ahead. Slowing his pace, he then rocketed in its direction with a flick of his tail. One powerful leap from the sea saw him transform back into human form, his hands grasping at the diving platform and pulling him on board.

Heaving in angry breaths, Logan grabbed a towel from the waiting pile and threw it around his waist. He strode away, searching the deck for his friends.

"Hey!" It was Flynn who found him, his smile vanishing at the sight of Logan's glower. "What's happened?"

"An oil slick." Logan's jaw tightened. "Sixty miles out from here."

"What?" Flynn glanced past him to the ocean.

"You heard me." Logan squeezed his hands into fists, pushing his nails into his palms. "Some imbecile has allowed gallons of the shit to seep into the sea, and the tide is pushing it toward shore."

"Not again." Flynn shook his head. "When will people ever learn?"

"Apparently not today," Logan growled. He was

usually a calm and happy man, but every now and again, something would happen to rile the beast in him, and seeing his beloved ocean denigrated in such gruesome style counted as one of those occasions. "Since we're stuck in Mexico for a few days, waiting for Devon's investigation into the Admiral's death to conclude, I'm going to figure out who's to blame and rain hellfire down on them."

"Must be a local rig." Flynn's gaze swept to the horizon as if he expected to see the offending platform.

"Maybe." Anger rose inside Logan in waves, making it difficult to think. "But someone's responsible, and I intend to find out who. Right now, there's no one out there at all. They're just permitting it to spread, and—" he slammed his fist into the railing, scarcely acknowledging the pain as it ricocheted to his shoulder.

"Hey." Flynn wandered to Logan, patting him on the shoulder. "We'll figure it out."

"Figure what out?"

Logan turned to see Mason striding in their direction. Based on his smug expression, he'd no doubt just enjoyed an afternoon session with his woman, Shiloh, and that was the cause of his apparent contentment. Logan's nostrils flared at the thought. It wasn't that he disliked Shiloh, or the other women Zak and Flynn had partnered with, but they were fast becoming a distraction from their mission. While Logan was out surveying the devastation, his friends were on board, living their lives between their legs.

"There's been a slick offshore." Flynn answered for him. "Logan just found it."

"Oh no." The light slipped from Mason's gaze in a heartbeat. "What can we do?"

A pang of guilt echoed in Logan's chest, reminding him that his resentment of the new status quo was unwarranted. Three of his closest friends may have introduced ladies into their lives, but it didn't stop them being his family. They were there for him, no matter what.

"I'm not sure." Logan turned to meet Mason's stare. "I'm going to get dressed and take *Top Secret* back to shore. Someone has to know who owns the local rig, and someone there will answer for what's happened."

"Let me come with you." Mason took a step forward. "We can cover more ground together."

"Thanks." Logan's lips twitched. "I appreciate it."

"Of course," Mason replied, his focus flitting to Flynn. "I'll take *Top Secret* back to the coast now. I know you and Devon will be heading to the hotel."

"Right." Flynn nodded as he approached Mason. "She has a meeting with her ensign, so I'll hang around and wait for her."

"Still worried about her safety?" Mason's eyebrow arched. "Even though that worm Schumacher is dead?"

They'd discovered the good news about Schumacher's untimely shooting the day before, and somehow, it still seemed too good to be true. The man had been the bane of their lives for so many years; imagining a future without his slimy interference was almost impossible.

"Yeah." Flynn shrugged. "I know she can look after herself, but we're dealing with some pretty dangerous guys—one of whom finished off Schumacher. I think caution is the best approach."

"I agree." Logan sighed, rubbing his temple with his hand. The last few weeks had brought one challenge after the next, and even though he was thrilled Schumacher was dead, Logan agreed with Flynn's appraisal—anyone audacious enough to have pulled the trigger was a threat to them all—as well as the Guardian Project they protected. The oil spill had just become the latest woe for him to tackle. "Until we figure this out, everyone should watch their backs."

Mason murmured his acquiescence before stalking back to the helm. A moment later, the powerful engine purred beneath them, and *Top Secret* cut through the waves.

∽

By the time they reached the shore, Nash and Zak had joined them on deck, their three ladies as thick as thieves in the main salon. Logan relayed what he'd encountered in the water, and all five of them agreed they should do something. Nash volunteered to join Flynn and Mason. In a time before romance had immersed the group, Mason and Nash hadn't always seen eye to eye, but concern for the greater good seemed to have healed any divisions. They'd find the owners of the rig soon enough and nail their sorry asses to the wall for what they'd done. The sooner they had crews out on the water, saving the marine life, the better.

It didn't take long to ascertain the company responsible. After seeing Flynn and Devon off, the three of them had headed to the company's local headquarters, leaving Shiloh on board *Top Secret* with Zak and Trinity. Haunted by the scenes he'd witnessed at sea earlier, Logan took the lead, rushing from their hired vehicle and surveying the gigantic tower block.

"This is where the oil company's based?" His voice conveyed his skepticism. "Seems like they're well in touch with the ecosystem they pollute." He rolled his eyes.

"What did you expect?" Nash scoffed. "It's always the same with these profit-focused corporations—income over ethics. Gotta pay the shareholders…"

"I know, but still…" Irritation swelled again as Logan recalled the appalling damage the oil had already done. "It doesn't leave the best first impression."

"Come on," Mason interrupted as he paced between them. "Enough chat. Let's go and talk to them."

Annoyed that his friend had taken the reins, Logan's stride increased. He tried to catch up with Mason, anxious to regain control. Hurrying in his direction, Logan's gaze settled on the huge revolving glass doors that shielded the foyer. They landed on a pair of shapely calves, striding from the doors, his concentration rising to the swell of their owner's hips and the cut of her executive suit. His pulse quickened as his attention rose higher, appreciating the view. The stranger wore her shoulder-length strawberry blonde tresses in soft curls, and her attention focused on her mission as she stalked away from them.

Logan's feet stopped, taking in the sight of her. He hadn't seen a woman as captivating for a long time.

"Hey, Casanova!" Mason chuckled, his gaze following where Logan's focus had landed. "We're here to find out about the slick, remember?"

Of course, Logan remembered. He'd been the one who'd spotted it, hadn't he? He'd been the one who'd witnessed the devastation.

"Sure." His attention flitted to Mason's smirk. "I'm right with you. Why don't you let me do the talking when we get inside?"

"No problem." Mason's lips twitched, but he didn't push the point.

Logan gestured for his two friends to go ahead of

him, waiting as their bulky frames entered the revolving door. As he waited for his turn, he glanced over his shoulder to get one more look at the mesmerizing blonde. Her heels halted by the roadside, and, as if she could sense the weight of his stare, she suddenly turned to meet his eyes. For one electrifying moment, their gazes locked, her green gaze burning into his memory. Then, as fast as she'd met his eyes, her attention returned to the car pulled up at the curb. Opening the door, she slipped into the back seat and was gone.

CHAPTER 2

Dallas

Dallas Miles could feel the weight of the moment as she stared back at hazel eyes focused on her. *Who was he? Why was he important?* The thoughts jangled in her mind as she tore her gaze away and got into the back seat of the car. Closing the door, she shook her head, not just to clear it of the man who had captured her attention, but that as a devout conservationist, she was being driven in a private car. The irony was not lost on her—ecologically friendly, it wasn't.

"Where to?" asked the driver.

"Posada del Océano."

Not even half an hour ago, she'd sat in the conference room, constrained in her conservative business suit at the top of the tallest building in La Paz, nursing a beer as she'd stared out toward the northwest to where she knew the Sea of Cortez lay waiting. She had no idea what the fuck they were doing standing around while deadly oil leaked once again into a delicate ecosystem. Oh yeah, she'd been waiting for all the big boys to fondle themselves.

Sighing, she took a long draw on her beer, wondering yet again how a rabid environmentalist had ended up working for an oil company. Be part of the solution, they said. At least that's what she'd told herself when she'd taken their hiring bonus and big salary right out of college. It all seemed so long ago and so very far away. The company's headquarters were in Houston, not far from the city where she'd been born and for which she was named. La Paz and this spill seemed to be a lifetime away from the girl who had wanted to save the world from itself.

"Dallas? You with us? Anything to add?" Brock Petrie said, one of the VPs from the company.

She turned around to eye the room full of old men. Well, not truly old, but a lot older than her.

"Nothing other than wondering why you're all keeping me here while you play with your dicks. I need to get out to the rig to see how much damage we've done. More importantly, I need to figure out how to stop the damn leak." She slammed her beer on the table. "Fuck it. You guys figure out how to spin it or who to blame. I'm going to go see what we can do to fix it."

She didn't wait for an answer or stop as the old men recovered from their shock.

"I think they want you to come back." One of the receptionists feigned a smile.

Dallas pushed the button for the elevator, stepping in as the doors opened and hitting the down button. Just before the doors closed, she mirrored the woman's expression.

"Well, people in hell want ice water, but that don't mean they get it."

Dallas glanced out the back window toward the skyscraper, unbuttoning her suit jacket and pulling at the silk tank she wore underneath. God, she hated meetings like that. The man who seemed riveted in her mind was no longer there but trying to forget the intensity of the moment was far more difficult than it should be. Too long without a man in her life—that was the problem. *No*, whispered the little voice inside her head. The problem was never having found the right man at all.

She didn't wait for the driver to get out and open her door. As soon as the luxury town car glided to a stop, Dallas was out of the car and striding into the hotel. Her cell phone rang. Pulling it from her purse, she glanced at the caller ID—Petrie—she snorted. She didn't care. She knew he was calling to either berate her for walking out of the meeting or to tell her to calm down and that they could talk it through. Problem was, she wasn't at all sorry she'd walked out on that group of masturbatory old men, and she had no intention of calming down.

She stopped at the front desk. "Could you arrange for me to get a vehicle—something like a Jeep—four-wheel drive and serviceable? Nothing flashy."

"Ms. Miles? Your company has two of the hotel's town cars at your disposal..." said Alejandro, the head of client services in the luxury hotel.

Suddenly, all the pomp and circumstance of her life bore down on her like an anchor being lowered into the ocean, threatening to drown her and eradicate all of her dreams and ideals. All she wanted to do was get her things, get to the rig, and figure out what the hell was going on. Had their new failsafe system failed? The thought gnawed at her gut.

"I know, but I don't want to tie up one of those cars, and I need to have something that can go offroad."

"I can have something here within half an hour."

The man was good at his job. "Thank you, Alejandro. That would be great."

She headed to the bank of elevators and pushed the button to take her up to her luxury suite—again, not the best use of the corporation's money. They needed to spend more on safer drilling and spill containment systems. As the elevator doors closed, she had to admit the idea of the men in the board room's junk made her throw up a little in her mouth, and that made her smile. Apparently, she hadn't yet learned to stomach all the wrinkled and gross things.

Entering her room, she stripped out of the corporate costume she was forced to wear to meetings. She grabbed her duffle as well as leggings and t-shirts and stuffed them into her bag. Pulling on jeans, a baggy,

V-neck t-shirt, and running shoes, she swept through the room, ensuring she had everything she'd need for a couple of days. Grabbing her hobo bag and the duffle, she took the elevator back down to the lobby where Alejandro was waiting for her, keys in hand.

"They just dropped it off," he said, proudly escorting her outside.

Dallas had to bite her lip. She'd been expecting a small Jeep or crossover of some kind, preferably open topped or at least with a sunroof. Black or white in color with not a lot of optional equipment. Something safe, sturdy, and workmanlike. What she got was probably the silliest vehicle she'd ever seen—it was open top, all right, but nothing came close to simply serviceable. It was a street-legal, metallic baby blue dune buggy that she was sure had every luxury option known to mankind.

"Thank you so much," she replied, taking the keys.

Alejandro took her duffle, strapping it in behind the seat, and opened the driver's side door. "Have a safe drive, Ms. Miles."

"Thanks again." Her voice was cheery as she pulled away from the hotel and out onto the busy street.

Finding a place to pull over, she paired her phone with the Bluetooth in the vehicle, then punched in a destination for a small boat rental company. Her phone trilled again. Seeing it was Petric, Dallas ignored it, pulled up a music streaming service, and headed toward the Sea of Cortez.

She just hoped she wasn't too late to head off an environmental disaster that would give new meaning to the word disaster, heading north along the coast. Unbidden, the man she'd seen staring at her as she left the company's offices in La Paz returned to plague and tantalize her. Hazel eyes—how had she known their color? They were too far apart for her to have seen that clearly, but instinctively, she knew they were.

Tall, broad-shouldered, fair-haired, and leanly muscular. He'd been gorgeous with his slightly longer, wind-tousled hair. It looked as though he'd just been for a long swim and had thrown on his clothes to head into the city or just gotten out of bed from a particularly good romp. His jeans had fit his ass nicely, and she'd been able to discern its round, firm fullness. Dallas laughed at herself. She really did have sex on the brain. No, that wasn't right. She didn't just have sex on the brain. She had sex with that man—who she most likely would never see again—on the brain.

No matter how hard she tried, she couldn't seem to vanquish the image of the man she'd seen as she was leaving the building. He seemed to have touched something deep inside her, tearing away her carefully constructed, mind-numbing but successful life. There was something about him—a wild and untamable spirit she sensed inside him. Something she'd forsaken in order to leave the trailer park where she'd been raised behind her once and for all.

On the radio, Bruce Springsteen began growling the lyrics to his song, *I'm on Fire*.

"You and me both, Bruce." She blew out a breath. "You and me both."

CHAPTER 3

Logan

Stalking from the glass-fronted building, Logan's hands balled into fists. "Well, that was a complete waste of time."

"Usual corporate bullshit." Mason snarled as they headed away from the oil company, their long paces elongated by the collective fury. "We should have known what their response would be."

"I know, but still." Logan shook his head. He couldn't believe the cavalier attitude of the guys who worked there. Frankly, he wanted to turn on his heel and see if he couldn't *persuade* them to care a little more. "I didn't expect them to be such morons."

"They said they've dispatched someone to start the cleanup." Flynn's tone was hesitant. "A woman by the name of Miles. That's something."

"It's not enough." Logan turned his face toward

the sun, struggling to contain the rage resurfacing within him. "The oil's been out there for hours. God only knows how much damage it's already done."

"I know." Flynn patted him on the shoulder. "But it's a start. Apparently, this woman is the best in the business."

"They would say that," Logan started, but an abrupt thought halted his sentence. A sudden image of the strawberry blonde he'd seen earlier as she stalked from the building filled his mind. He had no way of knowing that she was the woman Flynn was talking about, but something—an innate and rarely ignored instinct—told him that she was.

"Logan?" Mason's tone was inquiring. "What were you going to say?"

"Nothing." Logan exhaled. "I need to get back out there and see how far the oil has spread."

"You need to be careful," Mason warned. "I know we can dive under the slick, but it would be better to avoid it altogether."

"I have to *do something*."

Logan forced the words out between gritted teeth. Mason and Flynn were like family to him, and he didn't want to argue, but he seemed to be the one who was most concerned about the incident. That's not to say that the others didn't care, but it was clear Logan cared more. His brow knitted. Why had the spill affected him so badly? It was hardly the first of its kind and, sadly, it was unlikely to be the last.

"Okay, just take it easy." Mason smiled. "I understand, Logan, truly, but there's a limit to what we can achieve. Once we're in the water, we're limited in what our sharks can accomplish."

Logan's brow rose. It was odd to hear any of them speaking about their shark as if it were an obstacle, but he understood what Mason meant. Being in the water meant they lost the privilege of their arms and hands, which would make helping with the clean up a much more difficult task.

"I'm still going back."

Logan heard the petulance in his voice but didn't care. He had to know something was being done out there. Whoever this Miles woman was, she was only one person. Based on what he'd seen earlier, it would take a huge effort to save the aquatic mammals and seabirds who had probably already fallen foul to the crawling black slime.

"How about we stop by on route to the Kracken?" Flynn suggested.

"Fine," Logan agreed, keen to avoid further confrontation with his friends.

As far as he was concerned, the sooner they got back to *Top Secret* and into the water, the better.

∾

It took a frustrating quantity of time before the ocean enveloped Logan's senses again, but he felt instantly better just for diving into its cooling depths. Propelling himself through the water, Logan didn't wait for the others. Using his speed as the fastest shark in the sea, he raced through the waves in the direction of the slick.

His senses alerted him as the pollution neared, cautioning of the threat to come, and it didn't take long to discover why. Rising to the surface, his snout took in the air, but rather than the fresh sea breeze he usually enjoyed, the wind was filled with the noxious odor of oil.

Jesus. Logan scanned the area, sickened to see the extent of the slick's coverage. *It's going to take a supreme effort to clean this up.*

The sound of an engine drew his attention, and, turning, he noticed a small vessel cutting through the blackened water. Inching as close as the spill would allow, he caught sight of the boom as they started to try to contain the spill. So, someone was here, trying to help. The idea burgeoned, offering what felt like the first bloom of hope for hours, but from this distance, it was impossible to see who was at the helm.

He dove below, following the sound until he was closer to the boat. Finding a small break in the slick, Logan rose, breaking the surface.

"Move the boom into position!" A female voice broke through the air. "Quickly!"

Bobbing between two pools of the perilous pollution, Logan waited, listening for more.

"Christ, come on, you guys." Her irritation was easy to hear. "We've got to move faster than this."

"This is how it works, Ms. Miles."

Logan caught the faint response on the wind.

"Containing the oil takes time."

"I know, I know," came the vexed female reply. "I just wish we could do more." Her voice grew louder, and glancing up, Logan could see the woman at the side of the vessel. Her small hands clutched the rail, gripping it as if she intended to take out all her frustrations on the metal pole. "We need to do better than this."

This time, her voice wasn't loud enough for her colleagues to hear, but Logan heard it. Just below the surface of the water, he was listening to every word, but as he took in the sight of her exasperation, something else hit him. It was the same woman he'd spotted at the oil company, the one with the gorgeous strawberry blonde curls and vivid green eyes. Logan would have recognized her anywhere. So, the mesmerizing stranger was Ms. Miles? That was interesting…

"Hey?"

Peering up, he realized she had seen him in the water.

"Is that a shark?" She tilted her head as though talking to herself, leaning closer to the water. "Hey, buddy, what are you doing down there? You have to get away from the slick." She flicked her wrist at him, as if shooing him away, a gesture that curled his lips. The notion of such a tantalizing woman telling him to scram was as amusing as it was disappointing.

Checking his proximity to the sliding slick, he edged closer to the boat, bumping its side gently. Logan didn't really know what he wanted to convey to the beautiful blonde above. He only wanted to let her know he was okay, that he appreciated the effort she was overseeing. Although, if, as the jerks at the oil company had stated, she worked for the corporation who'd caused the spill, his growing attachment to the intoxicating stranger might prove to be a conflict of interest.

"What are you doing?" She laughed, revealing a row of stunning white teeth, and then, as if a new thought had occurred, her brow creased. "Are you hurt?"

Logan stared at her, desperate to communicate properly, yet aware that answering her would be an utterly reckless act, potentially putting the entire Guardian Project at risk. Eyeing her worried expression, he watched as two men rushed up behind her.

"That's a big shark." One commented. "Is it stuck in the slick?"

"I don't think so." The blonde half smiled as Logan swam away from the vessel. "Seems like he's trying to tell us something."

"Maybe one of his pals got stuck?" The other guy smirked, as if there was something hilarious about either the prospect or the concept of sharks having friends. "What kind of shark is it?"

"Could be a Great White?" proffered the first.

"It's a Mako." Miles' voice had conviction. "Jesus, don't you guys know anything about sea life?"

Logan's interest swelled at the way she dressed her colleague down. He had to meet this woman.

"Not much." The first guy shrugged. "I'm just paid to work the rig."

"You'd best get on with it then." Her tone oozed contempt, and from the depths, Logan watched as the two men slunk away.

"You'd better go too." Her voice was softer as she called down to him, though she couldn't possibly have known he would understand. "It's not safe for you here, little guy."

Logan didn't appreciate her patronizing tone, but glancing left and right, he realized she was right. The slick was drawing closer on all sides. With one last look at her pretty face, he headed below, diving beneath the oil as he re-routed to the Kracken.

Rocketing through the waves, the image of Miles stayed in his mind, taunting him as the old wreck neared. Two things were certain as he sped through the water. He had to meet her, had to find the woman on land and speak with her. The second thought that lingered as the sea rushed over his gills was that when he found her, he'd make her understand there was nothing *little* about Logan Knight.

CHAPTER 4

Dallas

Normally, being at sea refreshed her spirit and made her feel as if selling her soul to the devil meant at least the devil had a soul. But the smell of the oil, as well as her anger at those who had allowed it to happen and the team they had dispatched to try to contain the spill was so intense, it was making her nauseous.

She couldn't decide what she wanted to do first—throw up or punch the leader of the containment crew in the nose. The guy was an idiot, and worse, he was an idiot that didn't give a damn. When she'd arrived on the rig, they had yet to install the boom, and he was literally sitting on his ass having a donut and drinking coffee.

It had taken Dallas two hours to get from the hotel to the rig—a little less than an hour up the coast and then an hour by boat—two hours, and when she'd arrived, nothing had been done.

She could smell the spill long before she could see it. It permeated the air with its sick, industrial odor. She'd been told a crew had already been dispatched. What the hell were they doing? She couldn't hear any boat other than hers, and in order to get the boom in place, they needed to be out there doing it. The damn thing wouldn't install itself.

As she approached the rig, she could see that her ears hadn't deceived her. Absolutely nothing was being done. As she watched, she could see the idiots hadn't even shut down the rig. She knew that most of the guys who actually worked a rig hadn't done much more than graduate high school, if that, but it didn't take an advanced degree to know that if the rig was spilling oil, you needed to shut it down.

Dallas pulled the boat up to the platform's entrance and tied off. Where the fuck was everybody? Nobody came to see who was tying up to, much less getting on the rig? Damn. For all they knew, she could be a terrorist or a pirate or a smuggler come to do some harm. She climbed the ladder from the landing platform to the main deck and headed for the wheelhouse to speak to whoever was in charge.

From the time she tied up the speedboat until she threw open the door of the wheelhouse, not one person challenged her. In fact, she didn't see anyone. Surely, they hadn't just abandoned the rig, had they?

Once she had the door open, she found the foreman of the rig and the head of the containment crew sitting with their feet propped up, coffee mugs in hand, and a box of donuts sitting between them.

"What the fuck is wrong with you?" she roared.

The rig's foreman, whose chair had been leaned back on two legs, at least had the good grace to be startled and fall off his chair. The man she assumed was head of the cleanup crew merely gazed at her over the rim of his coffee mug, his eyes lustily taking in her figure.

"Who might you be, little lady?" His eyebrow rose with his insolent drawl.

"I'm the little lady who's going to kick your balls up around your teeth." She pointed to the foreman, who was still sitting on the ground. "Shut the goddamn rig down. You're just pumping more oil into the ocean. Do you even know where the leak is?"

"There's no need to talk to Barney that way," said the man still sitting in the chair.

"I've got plenty of reasons," Dallas snarled before turning to Barney, "Why are you still sitting there? Shut the goddamn rig down now!" Turning back to the man with the mug. "I'm assuming you work with the cleanup crew when you bother to work?"

"Now see here," he said, coming to his feet as Barney continued to stare at them.

"Barney, get your ass in gear."

Finally, Barney managed to scramble up off the floor.

"Barney, there's no need to jump just because this girl tells you to."

"Sure, there is," said Dallas. "*This girl* is in charge of this operation, and when *this girl* says jump, *this girl* expects people to ask how high as their feet leave the floor. And you are?"

"I'm Pete Costas. I'm the head of the cleanup crew."

"Not anymore, you aren't." She folded her arms across her chest. "You're off the rig, and I'll be filing a recommendation that your ass is fired from the company."

"Who are you?" bellowed Pete.

Dallas smiled. Poor Pete had no idea how bad it was when she smiled like that. "I'm the ball-busting bitch they send in to try to mitigate disasters like this."

"Dallas Miles," whispered Barney.

Dallas smiled sweetly at him. "I understand they tell rig foremen that the last person they ever want to see mounting their platform is me." Barney nodded. "They're right, and they didn't exaggerate about what a truly nasty person I can be. Shut down the rig. Now."

"The company sent me out here," started Pete.

"Not to sit on your ass eating donuts. And why are you still on my rig? I meant it. Get on that cheap ass boat you had tied off and leave."

"You listen up, missy," he snarled. "If I leave, so does my crew."

"And that would be a problem, why?" she asked sarcastically. "As far as I can see, they haven't done jack shit. The crew isn't going to have much to do with the rig shut down, so I'll use them to get this mess cleaned up." She turned back toward Barney, who was finally getting the rig shut down. "Make sure Pete and his crew are gone in the next half hour, then I want to see our guys on the platform."

"You'd better leave, Pete," Barney suggested.

"You just gonna do what this bitch tells you?" asked Pete belligerently.

"Yeah," said Barney. "She's one of the company's muckety mucks, and she's right. One of the first things you hear coming to work for the company is the last person you want coming aboard the rig is her."

"Barney, I take it we have a security team?" Dallas asked; Barney nodded. "Get the head of the team to bring a couple of guys and escort Pete here and his people to their boat. I want them off the rig. I'm going to go check the status of the emergency containment equipment, then I'll see what we need from the mainland."

"Yes, ma'am," he said as Dallas headed out the door.

"We're not done here," sputtered Pete, who finally

seemed to be grasping the fact that she was taking over.

"I'm not, but you are. I'm just getting started."

Two hours later, Pete and his erstwhile crew had been dispatched and were headed back to shore. Three of them had approached her, apologized, and asked if they could work freelance. Barney seemed to have gotten with the program and said they had tried to do more, but Pete had stopped them. She'd talked to the rig's crew and outlined her plan, at least for the remainder of the day, to start to contain the spill. She had to say, they seemed onboard. It would be better to have a cleanup crew of experienced guys, but she would make do with what she had. At least those still aboard the rig seemed to want to get the oil cleaned up. She fought down the urge to vomit—there was just so much oil, and so much damage had already been done.

They worked quickly and efficiently to deploy the boom so at least the oil wouldn't spread, and with the rig shut down, it wasn't actively pumping the pollutant into the water. Dallas was working on trying to contain her anger, which she had to admit to herself, was a bit over-the-top, even for her. She chalked it up to Pete's belligerent and uncaring manner and not taking any time for herself in the past few months.

She snorted at her own assessment—taking enough time? Few months? The fact was she hadn't even had an orgasm in the past six months and hadn't had sex with a man in more like eighteen. God, that was pathetic and really was starting to affect her work… and everything else in her life. Not much she could do about it today or until this spill was taken care of. But she promised herself she'd try to find someone—maybe the gorgeous man she'd seen heading into the company's headquarters—to take care of that for her. Or barring that, a good long session with a vibrator.

Looking out over the oozing black mass, she clutched the railing to keep from screaming. How the fuck had this been allowed to happen? Maintenance issues? Defective parts? Human error? Sabotage? The fact that the latter was a real possibility didn't help improve her mood.

She saw the dorsal fin of what appeared to be a Shortfin Mako cut through the water.

"Hey, buddy," she called. "What are you doing down there? You have to get away from the slick."

She flicked her wrist at him to shoo him away and then realized she was talking to a fish—a very large fish with razor-sharp teeth—but a fish *as if* he could understand her.

He bumped up against the boat as if he'd understood her warning or was trying to tell her something. That was ridiculous. It was a shark, for heaven's sake. A sleek, lightning-fast shark, but still not like he was going to tell her where the leak was, how extensive the damage from the spill was, or how bad the damage was going to be.

She was relieved when he sank below the oil-soaked surface to the depths of the sea below. Taking a deep breath, she turned back toward the equipment container. Once the boom was in place and stabilized, they would start working the spill with the skimmer. She headed down to her own boat to get her duffle and monitoring equipment. One of the first things she needed to do was see how deep the slick was. If it was thick enough, they could do a controlled burn. It was a noxious process, and everyone would need the appropriate safety gear but at least with the boom in place, she could keep the damn thing from spreading.

Thinking of burning the slick, she smiled as she thought how appropriate Springsteen's *I'm on Fire* was to a lot of aspects of her life.

CHAPTER 5

Logan

Logan stopped back at the slick on his way from the Kracken to *Top Secret*. He couldn't help himself. He had to know what was happening with the oil—the image of its clawing fingers haunting him in the back of his mind while he swam circuits around the sunken wreck. More than that, though, the recollection which haunted him was the woman he'd seen on the recovery vessel.

Who was she? Yes, he knew her second name and assumed she worked for the oil company—but that wasn't what he meant. He wondered, who was she really? What drove her? What kept her up at night and, if he was being honest with himself, Logan wanted to discover how *he* could become that man.

Approaching the location, he rose to the surface,

assessing the area in the growing morning light. Yes, there was still pollution, but he had to admit, the initial containment had done a decent job. Satisfied, he dove deep into the water, thoughts of the captivating strawberry blonde fueling him as he rocketed toward the yacht. Logan didn't know much about the woman, but it seemed she'd started the recovery process, and that gave him hope. Hope that the marine life wouldn't be totally pulverized by the slick and hope that he could overlook her apparent employment and get to know who she was.

Leaping from the water, he transformed into his human form and was smiling as he climbed on deck. He wrapped his towel around his middle as he strode to the salon.

"Where have you been?" Nash's eyebrow arched. "You left before me and are always the fastest swimmer."

"I stopped by the slick." He met Nash's eyes.

"Again?"

"I had to know what was happening." Logan's tone was defensive, though he didn't know why. He didn't have to justify his decision to Nash… or anyone else.

"And?"

"Most of it has been contained." Logan reached for a glass and headed for the jug of fresh water. Their nightly patrols always left him horrendously thirsty. Pouring himself a glass, he drained the entirety before turning back to his friend. "Hopefully, they'll continue working on it today."

"You sure have a hard-on for this oil slick." Zak's sardonic tone drew Logan's attention. "Are you sure there isn't more to it than just the environmental hazard?"

"Isn't being concerned about the state of the ocean enough?" Logan intentionally avoided his question. Zak's knowing smirk was affecting him more than he wanted to admit.

"Naturally." Zak's grin grew, revealing a row of near-perfect white teeth. "It's just I heard how intrigued you were about the blonde who's in charge of the spill, and I wondered if she might be the impetus."

"I don't even know her." Logan slammed down the glass, unreasonably irritated that Zak had been able to read him so easily. "Anyway, so what if she is?" His full focus was on Zak now. "You, Flynn, and Mason have ladies in tow. Why shouldn't Nash and I have some fun?"

Zak's brow rose, and at that moment, Logan realized his response had only confirmed Zak's suspicions. Yes, Logan had designs on the strawberry blonde. Why else would he have taken Zak's bait and overreacted?

"I think you should." Zak's expression was serious.

"I can't speak for Mason and Flynn, but I'm much calmer and happier now I have Trinity in my life. Maybe a woman is just the tonic you need too?

"I'm going for a shower." Logan couldn't bear any more of Zak's psychoanalysis. He loved the guy but didn't need Zak to life coach him. Blowing out a breath, he headed past Zak's leer for the exit.

"Listen, a few of us are heading back to shore later," Zak went on. "Devon has a meeting, and we thought we could find somewhere to eat. You're welcome to join us."

"What time?" Logan glanced over his shoulder.

"Around six." Zak shrugged. "Nothing's fixed, but we're thinking an early dinner and a couple of drinks before patrol."

"Sure." Logan forced himself to smile, the gesture relieving some of the tension he'd held in his shoulders. He didn't know why he was so grouchy with Zak. It was hardly his friend's fault that Logan was desperate to get laid. "Thanks for the invite."

∼

Cradling his cold beer later that day, Logan couldn't decide why he'd agreed to come along. His gaze scanned the table, taking in the scene. Three of his closest friends—all of whom were part of the Guardian Project—were entangled with their new lovers in the small local restaurant they'd found, each as besotted as the next. Tearing his attention from the three snuggling couples, he met Nash's eyes. Nash's bullish expression conveyed a similar conclusion—it was getting tougher to be single in the group. Logan adored every man sitting at the table and would give his life to protect any of them but having to witness their developing happily ever afters was increasingly difficult to swallow.

Logan glanced down at the bottle in his hand, noticing it was nearly empty. "Fancy another?" He lowered his voice so that only Nash would hear him.

"Sure." Nash's cynical tone assured Logan that he wasn't the only one who was underwhelmed by all the burgeoning romance. "You can get them, though. I need to find the men's room."

"No problem." Logan rose from the table and considered asking the others if they needed more drinks, but the whispered chats and roaming hands convinced him they would be fine. He watched Nash walk to the end of the restaurant before wandering toward the small bar.

"Can I help you?" A petite brunette smiled at his approach, and fleetingly, he considered turning on the charm and going back to her. Returning her smile, his lackluster desire faded. The truth was, there was only one woman on his mind, and her strawberry blonde curls were nowhere to be seen.

"Two beers, please."

"Shall I add them to your tab?" she asked, gesturing to their table behind him.

"Sure."

Logan resisted the urge to turn around and acknowledge the table, knowing already that he'd find three loved-up couples making eyes at each other. Shit, he had to let this resentment go. These people were his best friends, and if they'd found happiness with amazing women, Logan should be happy for them. Even to him, this growing petulance was starting to wear thin.

"I'll bring them to your table," she suggested.

"No, thanks," he replied. "I'll wait and save you the trouble."

"Whatever you like." Turning, she wandered to the refrigerator in search of the beer.

"I'll have one of those as well, Alicia."

Logan tensed at the female voice behind him, peering over his shoulder to acknowledge its owner. His heart raced when his gaze landed on the exact strawberry blonde who'd been dancing through his mind all day—the same woman he'd seen at the slick and departing the oil company.

"Sure thing, Dallas." The bartender, Alicia, responded with her trademark smile, but Logan barely noticed. Every fiber of his being was attuned to the diminutive blonde as she stood at the bar beside him.

Dallas? Was that her name?

"Hi there." Meeting his intense gaze, her tone spoke of a woman who was used to men gawking. Based on how beautiful she was, Logan wasn't surprised. "I hope you don't mind me piggybacking your order."

An image of her piggybacking him filled Logan's mind, and his balls tightened at the enticing prospect.

"Help yourself." He signaled to Alicia as she rose and returned with the beers. "I'm happy to help."

Dallas had the most mesmerizing eyes, and for a split second, Logan was lost in them. "Thanks." She reached for one of the bottles, slipping her free hand into her pocket and pulling out a ten-dollar bill.

"Please, let me get this for you." Logan watched her reactions carefully. He didn't want to offend her, but this was his first chance to actually engage the girl who'd piqued his interest.

"I don't usually allow strange men to buy me drinks." She grinned, running her tongue across her teeth in the most brazen display of provocation Logan had ever seen.

Fuck. Was there actually electricity sparking between them, or was it all only happening in his head?

"Why not make an exception? I promise I won't bite." His lips curled at the quip. She'd never understand it, but it still amused him. "I can be a gentleman."

"Enjoy!" Noticing the interaction between the two of them, Alicia retreated with a chuckle. Left alone at the bar, Dallas leaned closer, her voice lowering as if she only wanted Logan to hear what came next.

"But what if I don't want you to be a gentleman?"

CHAPTER 6

Dallas

The thought of *oh my god, he's gorgeous* was almost immediately replaced by *oh my god, I want to fuck him,* soon followed by *oh my god, what am I doing?* She couldn't believe she'd found the guy from the building this morning. Sure, she'd come looking deliberately for some guy who even vaguely reminded her of him, so if she took him to bed, she could close her eyes and fantasize about him, but she hadn't actually expected to find the man himself.

"Well, that can be arranged if that's the lady's pleasure," he drawled. "Logan Knight, at your service."

"Are you all about a lady's pleasure?" she purred.

What the hell had gotten into her? She didn't behave like this. What she wanted to get into her was beginning to press against the front of his fly, and it looked to be an impressive something.

Logan put his two beers down—who was the second one for? Then took hers as well, setting all three on the bar and closing what little distance there was between them.

"Absolutely. Especially if she's interested in seeing to mine. Are you interested in seeing to my pleasure, Dallas?"

She let out a nervous little laugh. Every instinct for self-preservation told her to run like hell. This man was a predator—but not a sexual predator. No, she'd be willing to bet her next paycheck, which would be considerable, that he was all about protecting. She didn't know him and would most likely never see him again, so perhaps it was worth risking. After all, there had been a restless need riding her all day. Nothing ventured, nothing gained.

"With the right person, pleasure can be mutually assured… Sir."

The sexy smile got larger. "What constitutes the right person, Dallas?"

"Jesus, not you too," growled a bull of a man as he grabbed one of the beers. "I'll let the guys know you've checked out for the rest of the evening. Try to have your ass back to the boat before we need to head out."

The man stalked away.

"Your friend seems to know something I don't," she smiled.

Logan chuckled. It was a deep, rhythmic sound that rippled over her jangled nerves to soothe them as he took her hand in his, drawing her closer. He gave her hand a tug, and Dallas responded by moving closer—close enough that there was barely room for a breath between them.

"What my friend knows is that I saw you earlier today and have had you in my head ever since."

"Is that where you want me, Logan?"

"Logan?" he questioned, his voice taking on that velvety darkness that only a true Dom could conjure up.

Again, every instinct told her to run; her libido told her instincts to shut the fuck up.

"Sir," she amended.

Logan rubbed his thumb along the back of her hand. "Better. As for where I want you…" He leaned forward so that he was whispering in her ear. "In a bed where the walls are thick enough that I can make you scream, and no one will hear you."

If he was trying to scare her, he was going about it the wrong way.

"Are you going to make me scream, Sir?"

He grinned. "Good girl, and to answer your question, loudly and frequently."

"Is that supposed to frighten me, Sir?"

"No, baby. It's supposed to give you fair warning and get your juices flowing."

"Check and check," she purred.

He ran his tongue around the outer shell of her ear before giving the lobe a little nip. "Are you wet for me, Dallas?"

She couldn't believe this was going so well. She'd come to get laid by a nobody—someone reminiscent of Logan. It seemed, however, as if the man himself was more than ready to step up to the plate.

Before she could answer, a beefy hand landed on her shoulder, only shortly before the smell of his beer-soaked, putrid breath assailed her nostrils.

"Hey you, bitch!" Pete from the cleanup crew she'd tossed off the rig earlier today growled behind her. "You got me fired."

She didn't have time for this. She needed Pete to disappear. Dallas whirled on him before either he or Logan even had time to breathe, much less realize her intent. She brought her knee up into his groin with enough force that he staggered back before falling to his knees. The move had been instinctive, and fleetingly, she wondered how Logan might react to her aggressive mood.

What Dallas wasn't expecting was for his reaction to be an equally swift, stinging swat to her backside. She might have stumbled forward, save for the muscular arm wrapped around her waist.

"While I applaud the sentiment, baby." He was

right there behind her. "You don't knee guys in the groin when I'm around. If there's a problem, I'll handle it. Understand?"

"Uhm… yes, Sir."

"Good girl." He casually cupped her breast before pushing her behind him as Pete got to his feet and came toward them, only to be met by Logan's fist to his face, causing Pete to stumble backwards, landing on his ass. "I don't know who you are, asshole, and I don't much care. The lady is with me. Now, back off."

Pete looked up into Logan's face, and even though she couldn't see it as his back was turned to her, and she was enjoying the view of his muscular, rounded buttocks beneath his jeans, it must have scared Pete as he crab-crawled away from Logan.

"Logan," she said sharply. He turned back around, obviously surprised at her tone. She took his fist in her hands and brought it up to her mouth. "Did you hurt your hand, Sir?"

The look he gave her morphed into a purely sexual one as he grinned. "Not anything a kiss from you wouldn't make right."

She lowered her eyes, not sure if she was ready for the intensity of his heated gaze, as she kissed his knuckles. "Like this, Sir?"

"I think you can do better, baby."

Dallas ran her tongue over his fingers between the knuckle and the joint before whispering kisses across the same trail. "I can do a lot better, especially if the something offered is bigger than a finger."

She imagined that Logan's chuckle was the sound of sexual arousal. Forget moaning, groaning, and sighing. No, it was the amused, all alpha male sound that accompanied his sensual smile.

"I'll bet you can, and sometime before morning, I'll give you the opportunity to prove that."

She wasn't sure what she was expecting, but to be tossed over his shoulder and carried out of the bar to the cheers, jeers, and catcalls of the other patrons wasn't it. As they left the room and headed for the door, she allowed her head to just fall forward and hide her blushing cheeks in his back. Once outside, she raised herself up and tried to push off of him. His response was as quick as it was sharp—another hard smack to her ass. Hard enough that she could feel it keenly even through her jeans.

He carried her through the streets that led from the dockside tavern down to an enormous yacht and up the gangplank. From what she could see, the ship was luxurious and had biometric sensors to gain entry. She was carried down a long hallway.

"I can walk, you know," she argued, trying hard to sound a bit peeved or even a bit nervous—anything but what she was, wildly aroused.

"I'm sure you can, but I prefer to carry you." His reply was a throaty snarl. "The scent of your desire is intoxicating."

He opened one of the doors and carried her inside, closing it behind her and depositing her on a large bed that seemed to be decked out with a restraint system.

"We have some playrooms on board with all kinds of fun things, but right now, I just want you naked and on your knees."

"Logan…" she started, feeling as if she should make some token protest and then deciding to abandon the pretext. "I haven't been with anyone since my last physical, and I'm on birth control."

"When was your last physical?"

"More than six months…"

"No sex since then? My poor, sweet baby. We have a lot of time to make up for. I'm clean too."

She tried to think of something to say, but her thought process was interrupted.

"Why aren't you naked?" he growled seductively.

Dallas removed her clothes as quickly as possible so she could kneel on the floor. He hadn't said how he wanted her positioned, so she adopted a classic submissive pose—kneeling and rocked back, sitting on her heels, her hands placed on her thighs and her head forward.

"Very nice," he crooned, his pleasure evident in his voice. "Someone's had some training."

"Yes, Sir. I've worked on some oil rigs in the North Sea and frequented a club in Scotland and one in

England. Both had training programs for their submissives."

"Was that your introduction to the lifestyle?" He lifted her face with his finger under her chin.

"Yes, Sir."

"What attracted you to it?"

"The ability to lose myself in the purity of the exchange. I have a kind of high-pressure job, and it was getting to me. The first club I played at was the one in London, Baker Street, and it allowed me to find myself and a way to deal with the stress and not have to be in charge for a while. I found," she hesitated, looking for the right word, "peace."

"Good enough," he said, nodding. "I'm going to take care of you, Dallas. I'll take care of your needs, but first, I need some relief, and you're going to see to it."

A slow smile spread across her face. "Yes, Sir," she purred and waited to follow wherever he wanted to lead.

CHAPTER 7

Logan

She was magnificent on her knees, her soft curves as tantalizing as any Logan had ever seen. Starting a circuit around her body, he allowed one fingertip to stray into her mesmerizing blonde mane, curling her tresses around the digit.

"What's your safeword, baby?"

Excitement coursed through his system, tightening his balls in anticipation. It had been too long since he'd had the chance to play with a woman as ravishing as Dallas, and he intended to savor every second.

"I don't actually have one; I've just always used the stoplight system, so red, I guess, Sir." Her lips twitched as she met his eyes.

"That's fine. I know a lot of couples who use it as

it's easy to remember." He smiled, releasing the strands of her hair as he took a step away.

She offered him a furtive smile. "Anything else, Sir?"

"No. That should cover it." Unbuttoning his shirt, Logan wanted nothing more than to devour the gorgeous blonde on her knees. "How about you let your actions do the talking?"

"Certainly, Sir."

Tugging his shirt free from his pants, Logan lowered his zipper, releasing his eager cock. Dallas' face lit up at the sight of his erection.

"See anything you like, baby?"

"Yes, Sir." She licked her lips slowly, ensuring their gazes locked during her salacious display.

"Get over here and take care of it then."

He beckoned her forward with one finger, arousal swelling as she fell forward and crawled the short distance to where he stood. Rising on her knees, her focus flitted to his face before she took his cock in her hands. Easing his shaft along her palm, she flicked her tongue over his crown.

"Mouth only," he growled, frantic to steady his growing fervor. At this rate, she would topple him over the brink in record time.

"Yes, Sir." She smiled as her hands fell to the small of her back, her lips parting to receive more of his cock.

Logan watched while she worked her mouth up

and down his rod, taking him deep in her throat before coming up for air. The sensations as he filled her were intoxicating, her heat mingling with her invigorating scent to taunt him, pushing him closer to the edge of his climax.

"Jeez."

Clutching her hair, his fingers burrowed into her luxuriant tresses, allowing him to take control of the pace. Fisting her curly mane, he held her steady as he lunged into her mouth, pushing his cock right down her throat until there was nowhere else for him to go. Gagging around his intrusion, Dallas' eyes filled with water as she grappled with his hard length, and it was fucking sublime.

"That's incredible."

He eased away a little, giving her an opportunity to breathe before he plunged deep into her again. If Dallas' mouth was this good, he couldn't wait to sample the rest of her delectable body.

"I did tell you, Sir," she gasped, grinning as he drew away.

His cock was engorged and would soon be ready to spill his seed all over her glorious face. Easing his jeans from his hips and onto the floor, he stepped out of them as he inched closer. "You did," he agreed. "Lap at my balls, baby." His fingers tightened in her hair, guiding her forward. "Worship them."

Their gazes locked for the briefest moment, her

pupils dilating before she caught her lower lip between her white teeth.

"Yes, Sir." She buried her face into him, licking at his testicles as if her life depended on it.

Logan's desire surged at her submission. It was clear that not only was Dallas comfortable in her capitulation, but she reveled in it, too. The woman had blossomed since he'd brought her here and ordered her to strip. He couldn't wait to see more of her wonder, to know more of the delightful bud slowly unfurling before him.

"Oh yes," he enthused, relishing the feel of her hot tongue lapping at his balls. His cock pulsed above her, desperate for more of her attention. "I like that." Stroking the side of her cheek, he tipped her chin toward him, witnessing her devotion. "Do you like it too, baby?"

"So much, Sir." Heat pooled in her cheeks as she paused. "You have such a magnificent cock."

"It wants more of you," he told her. "But first, I'm going to paint your pretty face with my cum."

Her lips curled at his promise, and he directed the tip of his organ back to her lips, sliding past them and pounding her throat. Dallas groaned around him, her mewls building the tension at his core and combining with the hot, satisfying sensation created by her throat. Soon enough, he was on the precipice of the most perfect pleasure.

"Here we go, baby." Withdrawing from her mouth

with a huge trail of saliva, he pumped the first round of his cum over her nose and mouth. "Open wide."

Her lips parted obediently, her tongue waiting as he deposited the next wave of his orgasm there. Logan couldn't recall hedonism like it, his gratification more powerful than even he'd been expecting.

"Amazing." He caressed the side of her face as the final fragments of his climax washed over him. "You're wonderful." His finger trailed a line over her face, collecting the remnants of his passion and offering it to her.

She leaned forward, obliging him by sucking at the digit and cleaning his flesh. "Thank you, Sir."

"I think it's time for my lady's pleasure." Offering her his hand, Logan helped Dallas to her feet.

"It is my pleasure to serve you, Sir."

"I noticed." Snaking an arm around her delicious body, he drew her closer. "I adore your service, but I also want to tie you to that bed and gobble you up."

He motioned to the huge bed behind her, and she turned, following his gaze.

"That sounds tempting," she admitted. "But…" Her voice trailed away.

"But?" His brow rose. Logan hadn't been expecting any protest about his suggestion, but he was open to her feedback. "What do you need, beautiful?"

Capturing her chin between his thumb and forefinger, he drew her attention back to his face.

"I…" She blew out a breath as if she was struggling for the right words.

"Dallas." His tone deepened. "If there's something you need, then I expect you to tell me. Will a little punishment help lubricate your tongue?" His eyebrow arched at the irony of the question. Only a few minutes before, he had done just that himself.

Her eyes lit up at the threat—not exactly the reaction he'd anticipated. "Maybe, Sir."

"Hang on." He steered her toward the bed, towering over her as he went on. "Is that what's going on here? Do you need to be punished?"

She shifted her weight between her feet, the blush at her cheeks burning a little brighter. "It's been a long time since my last spanking, Sir."

Her eyes were full of apprehension and longing, though he didn't know why. If that was all she needed, she should have just said. Logan adored spanking a willing woman, and Dallas was close to perfection.

"How long, baby?" The hand at her chin tipped it north to fix her focus to his, while his free hand roamed to her entrancing ass. Christ, he couldn't wait to color it for her.

"Too long." Dallas practically sighed the words. "Maybe two years."

"Two years." He gasped theatrically, squeezing her backside. "That's far too long for a woman with your sexual appetite."

"Right." She threw him a nervous smile. "So, you see my problem, Sir?"

"I do, indeed, and I'm happy to help, but first, you're going to have to ask me."

"Ask you?" She nibbled at her lower lip again. Evidently, Dallas hadn't expected that demand. "Ask you what, Sir?"

"For what you need, baby."

Her brow creased as if the quandary was impossible to resolve, and then she smiled, the words he wanted spilling from her alluring lips. "Please, will you spank me, Sir?"

"You know I will." His recently satiated cock stirred at her breathy plea. "Your wish is my command."

CHAPTER 8

Dallas

This hadn't been what she'd been looking for when she walked into the bar. Oh sure, she'd wanted to get laid, but to find a truly dominant alpha male and to be able to give herself over to him? Finding that had never entered her mind. She knew this was no wannabe jerk who thought he was a Dom or only played at being one in a club. No, she sensed Logan was the real thing, and now he was going to give her what she'd been needing for far too long.

Life had been running at a whirlwind pace. There'd been no time to think, to breathe, to just be, and it had begun to wear thin. Dallas had long ago accepted that she had an aggressive streak but had learned to balance the trait by acknowledging and indulging her need to temper it with submission to the right man—even if for only a night. She'd given up the idea that a man like that would ever be a permanent fixture in her life. But for right now, at this moment, this man fulfilled every need or desire she had.

Logan sat down on the edge of the bed and guided her across his lap. His thighs were muscular, and she could feel his cock coming back to life as he settled her over his knee, placing his hand in the small of her back. Dallas shuddered as his other hand caressed her upturned buttocks.

"Easy, baby. I'll take care of you."

She believed him. Her day had been long, hard, and incredibly stressful. She needed the relief the spanking would afford her, and as she heard his breathing become deep and rhythmic, she realized he needed to spank her almost as much as she needed to be spanked.

As she let her body go limp over his lap, she felt the brief uptake of air as he lifted his hand to bring it down onto her rump with a resounding smack. Dallas expelled a moan, which ended in a sigh. This was exactly what she needed. The way his hand had connected with her ass in the bar when he told her he would deal with Pete had ignited this deep urgency to connect with him in this way.

She'd loved giving him what he needed when she went down on him, and she wanted desperately to have him bury that magnificent cock deep inside her, but she needed this as well. His hand rose and fell over and over, peppering her backside, covering the flesh evenly. This was a man who knew how to give a spanking. There was just enough sting to make it uncomfortable and inspire heat, morphing into a delicious pleasure that flowed through her body and connected them. Dallas had no doubt that he could also deliver a nasty discipline spanking if he thought it was warranted.

She lost count of the times his hand smacked her ass and was glad that he'd felt no need to have her count the strikes. He was giving her precisely what she needed; she sensed he needed it too. His strikes were gentler at the beginning, and she worried for the briefest moment that he wouldn't give her what was required, but that fear was soon abated. Logan's hand landed again and again, and she knew she would feel the aftereffects for a day or two.

As he slowed the rhythm of his blows, she didn't want it to end. Her backside was quick to inform her it was aching and tender. As if he'd heard her ass' complaint, the spanking itself was over. But instead of just treating it like some task he needed to accomplish, he soothed her heated flesh in order to give her time to just be.

Logan's hand eased between her parted legs, checking to ensure the spanking had done its job. It had; her pussy was weeping with arousal. He stroked her gently, relaxing her even further, letting her know she was in the hands of a man who knew just what he was doing. He caressed her silky skin, spreading the proof of her need all around, penetrating her with a single finger and making her moan.

"That's it. I've got you."

His finger slid deeper and deeper inside her while his thumb found her clit and pressed. His cock pulsed beneath her, reminding her there was more he could do for her. He played her pussy like a maestro played a cello, hitting all the right notes as the strings trembled at his touch. He eased her into her orgasm as her body stiffened and her breath caught, a fresh rush of arousal coating her sex and his hand.

"That's my good girl." He helped her from his lap and to stand on shaking legs.

Tugging her hair back, his mouth covered hers as his tongue surged in, sweeping through her mouth and igniting the embers left over from the climax he'd given her. He backed onto the bed, pulling her along with him, molding her body to his as she rose up, straddling his hips—her sex poised above his engorged cock. He grinned, and they both knew that she might be on top of him, but that wouldn't last long, and it meant nothing. He was dominant and would top her in whatever position they engaged.

Dallas smiled, completely at ease and totally aroused, hissing as his one hand connected smartly with her well-spanked backside. "Girls who tease get punished. Is that what you want?"

"No, Sir."

He pulled her into position, leading even from beneath her. His hands grasped her hips and then pulled her down onto his cock, inch by inch. She moaned as he impaled her, sliding her up and down on his dick. Logan rocked his hips, thrusting upward and watching her face as he drove home. Dallas shook from the feeling of lust as it washed over her.

Over and over, he guided her in the rhythm he wanted, letting her get just to the edge of the abyss but backing off so that she couldn't quite fly free. After frustrating her a third time and chuckling as he did so, she leaned forward, trying to pin him down so she could ride him properly and take what she needed.

"Unh uh," he said, grasping her waist, flipping her over onto her back, and taking control. "Legs around my waist."

Without thinking, she complied as he pounded into her. Over and over, he slammed into her, fucking her with a ruthless need to exert his command. Dallas clung to him, savoring the intensity of his possession and reveling in it—her body alive with ecstasy. She trembled beneath him, a slave to his pleasure. Her breath became rapid and thready, her moans morphing to whimpers as her orgasm rushed to the fore.

This time, he didn't pull back, simply hammered her pussy with renewed vigor as her body stiffened and she went careening over the edge into the abyss. He gave a hard, ferocious thrust deep, grinding his body against hers as her pussy greedily milked his cock, taking his second load of the night.

Logan grunted as he pumped her full of his cum, finally dropping onto her, burying his face in her neck, and giving her his full weight as he sighed. Dallas held him close and let him rest as she drifted in the soft atmosphere of absolute satisfaction.

Logan raised his head, smoothing the hair from her face before brushing his lips against hers. "Do I need to say it?" he asked.

"No, Sir. I shouldn't have tried to take over."

"And?"

"Sir?"

"If you ever do it again, I'll blister your ass, and you won't get to come for a week."

Dallas gulped. He wasn't joking, and not only did they both know he could do it, they also knew it wasn't an idle threat. Something thrilled inside her as she realized Logan didn't view this as a one-night stand. It might not mean forever, but it meant she could revel in the bliss a little longer.

"Yes, Sir. I'm sorry. I got greedy."

"You did." He smiled. "You need to know that I'll take care of all of your needs, including needing to be punished when you step out of line."

"Thank you, Sir," she said, kissing his strong jaw.

Logan settled back down on her, not seeing a need to withdraw. They laid together, neither willing to break the bond they'd found as they drifted off to sleep.

CHAPTER 9

Logan

He stirred early, reveling in the heat of Dallas' smooth skin before she woke. Eventually, his caresses roused her from her beauty sleep.

"Good morning." His lips curled up as her eyes blinked open.

"Good morning, Sir." Her brow rose. "Do I still need to use that title?"

"Do you like using it?" Logan suspected he already knew the answer, the bloom of heat at her cheeks confirming his deduction.

"Yes, Sir."

"Then you should." He trailed a finger along her arm, watching as goosebumps rose on her flesh.. "I didn't mean to wake you. It's just been too long since I awoke to anyone so beautiful."

"I was thinking the same." Her small hand rose to his jaw, her fingers grazing over his stubble.

"I need a shave." He caught her wrist gently. "Fancy a shower?"

"Is that an order, Sir?"

"Oh, absolutely." He grinned. "I always want you wet."

She chuckled as he rose, guiding them both to their feet. Drawing her knuckles to his lips, he brushed a kiss over her skin before he wandered to the nearby shower room.

"This is an amazing place." Dallas' gaze took in the breadth of the room.

"Thanks. I'm glad you like it." Logan's voice reverberated from the bathroom as the sound of running water rose from behind him. "Ready to join me?"

She padded over, and he sensed the weight of her stare as he strode under the water. Logan hoped she liked what she saw and that her aching pussy and backside were a testament to how much he'd appreciated her. Closing the short distance between them, he held out his hand, steadying her as she closed the cubicle door and wandered under the waterfall.

"I wanted to say thank you for last night." She turned back to meet his eyes. "It was everything I needed and more."

"You're more than welcome." The same dark glint she recognized from the night before gleamed in his gaze. "The pleasure was mutual. How's the wonderful ass this morning?" Logan grabbed it, squeezing her right cheek possessively. "Sore?"

"Nothing I can't handle, Sir." Dallas spun to face him, rising on her toes to kiss his jaw. "I liked the spanking."

"It seems like you need them regularly." His eyebrow arched as he handed her the bottle of shampoo. "And you haven't had anyone to scratch that itch for you."

"No," she admitted, taking the product and squeezing some into her palm. "It's been frustrating."

"It needn't be," he assured her. "I'm available to help." He smirked, adrenaline coursing at the idea of assisting such a magnificent woman with such a wonderful task.

"Really?" Her tone was breathy as she stepped under the torrent and washed her hair free from the suds. "You'd like to see me again?"

"Of course!" Was she mad? Hadn't she seen herself? Logan would have been happy to devour her every night for the rest of his life. Intelligent, submissive, and gorgeous—Dallas checked his every requirement. "I should be based here for a while."

"Are you here with work?" she asked as he shampooed his hair.

"That's right." He was inherently cagey about revealing too much about his mission, but his instincts told him he could trust Dallas. They had right from the start. "What about you? You work for the oil company, right?"

"That's right." Her eyes widened, as if she couldn't believe he knew so much about her. "How did you know?"

"I saw you at their headquarters." Logan grinned, resisting the urge to divulge that he'd also spotted her containing the latest spill when he'd been patrolling. It was way too soon to be unmasking more about his mutation. "I just assumed the rest."

"That's right." Her lips curled. "I remember. You were there with some of your friends from last night." She blushed, and Logan wondered if she was recalling how he'd swept her from her feet and carried her from the bar over his shoulder. He hoped so. He wanted her to remember who was in charge—who would always be in charge when she submitted to him.

"What's a lovely lady like you doing working for such a ruthless company?" He had no right to ask. Dallas' business was her own, and yet she seemed so unlike the usual type he associated with oil. Normally, they were interested in profits over people and had little patience for protecting the environment. That didn't match the concerned woman he'd witnessed on the ocean, clearly frustrated that she couldn't do more to skim away the spill.

"It's a long story." She blew out a sigh. "Though I

do sometimes wonder if I'm working for the wrong side."

"Perhaps the industry needs more people like you." He smiled, snaking an arm around her and drawing her close. "People who give a shit."

"I do my best." She craned her neck to meet his gaze. "It can be an uphill struggle."

"Is that why you're so tense, baby?"

"Maybe." She squirmed under the intensity of his stare. "Or maybe it's just the effect you have on me, Sir."

"Mmmm, I like that idea more." Leaning down, he captured her mouth, running one hand along her wet flesh to grab her ass as his lips claimed her.

"Sir." Dallas caught her lower lip between her teeth. "I'm distracting you from shaving."

"That's true." He chuckled, releasing her backside and running his fingertips through his stubble. "Think you can help me instead?"

"Help you shave?" Her blonde eyebrow rose. "Isn't that putting rather a lot of trust in me, Sir?"

"No more than asking me to put you over my knee and spank you." His cock throbbed at the sweet memory of their connection. "I do trust you, baby."

She smiled at his verdict and reached for his shaving foam and razor, he switched the shower settings so that the side sprinklers burst to life. They would keep the air warm without washing away the foam while she worked.

"Here." He handed her the can of foam. "Can you reach okay?"

"It might be better if you kneeled, Sir."

Logan sensed she was suppressing the urge to laugh.

"If you don't mind?"

Reaching for her hair, he tugged it hard, drawing her head back. "I'll kneel for you, baby. Just so long as you don't forget who makes the rules."

Dallas gasped at the change of tack, though her dilating pupils and pebbling nipples conveyed her true feelings about his show of authority.

"I won't forget, Sir."

"Tell me." He demanded, relishing the urgency in her tone.

"You make the rules, Sir."

"Good." Releasing her, he clutched his razor as he lowered to his knees. "Is this better?"

"Perfect."

She squeezed foam into her small, delicate palm, massaging it onto his face. Logan had an incredible view of her toned body from the shower floor, her beading tits tantalizing as she worked the product into place. He wanted to grab her and pin her to the ground while he rubbed his swelling shaft between those fabulous breasts. He wanted to come all over her pretty face and make her thank him for every drop. But handing her the razor, he also wanted to nurture this growing intimacy between them. Sex wasn't difficult to find, but the chemistry he and Dallas appeared to share was far rarer. It deserved to be cherished. His pleasure would wait.

"Are you sure you want me to do this?" Dallas hovered the blade by his face.

"I'm sure." He grasped her hip, stroking her skin as she went on. "Go ahead."

"Okay." Her voice was loaded with nerves as she drew the blade across the foam. "Is now a good time to tell you that I've never shaved another person before?"

He chuckled as she washed the foam under one of the nearby torrents. "It's just as well I believe in you then."

"I guess so." Shifting her position, she worked on the other side of his jaw. "You have such a handsome face, though, Sir. I wouldn't want to cut you."

"You won't." He met her eyes as she turned to wash the blade again. "I have every faith in you."

Tipping his chin gently, she worked under his jaw. He could have laughed at the concentration in her wondrous green eyes but didn't want to distract her. She was, after all, holding a blade to his throat.

"There." She smiled, nibbling her lower lip as she surveyed her effort. "I think that's all of it."

"Are you happy with your work?" He ran his fingers over his jaw, pleased but not surprised to find no evidence of any remaining hair.

"Yes, Sir." She shifted from one foot to the other like a naughty schoolgirl. "I hope you are, as well?"

"I'm sure I will be."

Reaching for the razor, Logan placed it in the corner of the shower before he drew her hot little body against him. From this angle, her scintillating tits were at almost the perfect height for his mouth. His erection surged as though it was cheering him on, urging him to take the teat between his lips.

"Now I get to reward you for all your hard work."

CHAPTER 10

Dallas

Logan latched on to her nipple and sucked as he pulled her body closer. Dallas arched her back, making herself available for whatever he might want. It was a curious feeling to be in a place she didn't have to think, just feel, and yet understand so much at the same time. Logan sucked harder, nipping at her taut tips, making them ache. It was as if her nipples were hardwired to her pussy, and each time he sucked, her pussy spasmed even though there was nothing there for it to clamp down on.

The water cascading over their bodies might have been warm—hot even—but Dallas shivered. Her need for the man she had just shaved raced through her system, sending jolts of electricity all along her nerve endings and lighting her up in a way she had never felt before. Her body burned, and she knew the only way to quench the thirst he had ignited was to feel his cock stroking her inner walls again and again until they both got the release they needed.

With any other man, Dallas would have taken control and gotten what she needed. Logan had already shown her that wouldn't work.

"Logan, please?" she moaned. "You said you wanted me wet, and I am."

"Hmmm," he said, as if considering whether it might be true.

His hand came up to cover her breast and push her back against the wall as he nuzzled his way down her body, licking and nipping as he went. When he reached the V of her thighs, he nosed her labia, inhaling deeply and giving her the briefest flick with his tongue.

"You aren't just wet, baby, you're soaked. I probably ought to do something about that."

There was a pounding on the door from the passageway into their room. Logan stood, turning off the shower, his cock pressed against her belly throbbing with need.

"What?" he shouted.

"Flynn and Devon are back. We're meeting in the salon. Get a move on," came a disembodied male voice from the other side.

"Copy," Logan called back.

Dallas could feel herself blushing furiously. They

hadn't been exactly quiet the night before. She tried to lean forward but was plastered back to the wall.

"Where do you think you're going?" he snarled as he skimmed up her body. "I'm a long way from being done with you."

"I have to get back to the rig."

"I'll take you, but I can't wait until tonight… and there will be a tonight, won't there?"

Logan didn't give her a chance to answer before he lowered his mouth to hers, his tongue darting out to run along the seam of her lips. Her body was alive with heat and need, and she knew she wouldn't deny him. Her lips parted, and his tongue surged in, sliding along hers and promising pleasure beyond measure.

He lifted her up, using the wall for leverage. "Wrap those gorgeous legs around my waist. I've got to be quick, but I've got to have you again. Someone will take you to the rig, and I'll pick you up tonight."

Before she could acquiesce, he pulled her down, his cock thrusting up into her in a single surge. Dallas' legs tightened around him, and she bit into the top of his shoulder to keep from screaming as she orgasmed.

Logan chuckled. "They can't hear us, baby, not unless we want them to."

God, she loved the way he filled her up, thrusting in and out, making her moan as she was trapped between the now cooling tile of the shower and the warmth of his body. He stroked her long and hard, driving into her with an intensity that left her breathless and clinging to him with a need she'd never known before.

Instinctively she knew that last night had changed everything. She didn't know anything at all about Logan, other than he was a dominant alpha male who knew how to spank and fuck, and she realized she didn't need to. Somehow, they were linked through space and time. It was as if she understood the core of who he was. All they had to do was catch up with what was happening in this lifetime.

He hammered her pussy with ruthless and singular intent. She wanted to fight for what she wanted but knew it would be futile. Logan would give her what she needed; she would just have to succumb and let go.

"Good girl. You take what I give."

He slammed into her with renewed vigor as he filled her up, retreated, and plunged back inside her. His breathing became ragged and in synchronized rhythm to hers as over and over he pounded into her until she came, craning her head back and howling with ecstasy. The sound reverberated around the bathroom, and she could barely hear his fierce growl as he drove in a final time and held himself hard against her as he emptied himself deep inside.

Dallas collapsed around him as he wrapped his hands under her ass and stepped out of the shower, carrying her into the bedroom, still impaled on his cock. He grabbed a couple of towels and didn't set her on her feet or uncouple from her until they were standing beside the bed. He dried her, running the soft towel along her even softer skin before drying himself.

"I need to take another shower if I'm going directly to the rig."

"Why?" he asked, leaning down to brush his lips past hers.

"Because I'm pretty sure at this point, I smell like I just had sex with you."

Logan inhaled deeply, a slow smile spreading across his face. "Baby, you smell exactly how I want you to—like a woman who belongs to the guy who just filled her pussy with his cum. Your cunt's going to be dripping all over the seam of those jeans of yours. Now be a good girl and get dressed. We'll get you something you can eat on the way. My guess is Shiloh will take you. She's Mason's woman. You'll like her. In fact, you'll like all of them."

Dallas pulled back. He was making an awful lot of assumptions. They'd had one night together. Granted, it had been spectacular, but the logical part of her brain questioned everything.

"Don't," he cautioned.

"Don't what?" she asked.

In the blink of an eye, his hand smacked her ass with serious intent. "That. I know we just met, but we both know that what happened last night wasn't just a one-time thing. You're going to get dressed, we'll get you something to eat, and Shiloh will take you to the rig. Tonight, I'll pick you up, and we can decide what we want to do. I'll put my number in your cell, and when you reach the rig, you text me that you're there safe and sound."

He made everything sound so simple.

"And if I don't agree?"

His grin was wicked. "If I had time, I would so make you regret even questioning it. But I don't. So, either you decide to accept what you know is true, or I'll send you to that rig not only filled with my cum, but with a bright red backside."

Dallas searched his face, sensing he wasn't making an empty threat. There was a ruthless streak that ran through Logan and called to a deep, dark part of her soul.

"This isn't easy for me."

It was becoming clear that as soon as she capitulated, he would be tender and loving.

"I know, baby, but I don't have time this morning to tease it all out. You know I'm right, though, don't you?"

Dallas looked into his handsome face. He was so earnest and so sure, and she knew the time for prevarication and second thoughts had passed the moment he'd tossed her over his shoulder last night and carried her from the bar.

"Don't you?" he repeated.

"Yes, Sir."

His smile transformed his face. He was certainly handsome, but there was also a brutal, angular quality that was softened when he smiled.

"That's my good girl. Now get dressed. We gotta get a move on."

He quickly pulled on a pair of jeans and then grabbed her cell phone to enter his number into the contacts. She laughed when she saw how he'd listed himself. *Sir*.

Logan led her up to the galley, where a dainty woman with black hair and grey eyes handed her what looked and smelled like the most heavenly breakfast burrito ever made.

"Trinity," she said by way of introduction and handed her a second one.

"Dallas."

Trinity turned to Logan. "Shiloh's got the boat ready." She handed Logan two mugs of coffee. "Shiloh took cream and sugar up with her. Shake a leg, lover boy. Devon found something." Turning back to Dallas. "Nice to meet you. I'm sure we'll see each other again."

"I hope so," Dallas replied, realizing she meant it.

Logan held the two mugs in one hand and used the other to steer her topside and to the stern of the yacht. He helped her down onto a diving platform, handed the coffee to a stunning red head, who grinned at him, then helped Dallas onboard. He took her face in his hands and gave her a deep, lingering kiss that wound its way all around her as if he had pulled her close.

"I'll pick you up at the rig at seven unless you call me to come get you sooner. Try not to fret. It'll be all right. Tell her it'll be all right, Shiloh."

"I'll do no such thing," quipped the redhead. "I'm going to tell her to run like hell and stay as far away from the ocean as she can."

"You do, and I'll tattle to Mason on you."

"Well, shit." Shiloh laughed. "You're no fun at all."

Logan hugged Dallas close. "I don't think Dallas would agree with you, would you, baby?"

Normally this kind of banter made Dallas feel awkward, but it didn't this time.

"By the way, Shiloh, this is Dallas. Dallas, this is Shiloh. You two behave."

"See?" sassed Shiloh. "No fun at all."

Logan hopped back up out of the boat and wagged his finger at her. "Don't you be leading my woman astray."

"What makes you think she'd be the one doing the leading?" teased Dallas.

Shiloh pushed the throttle forward and swung the small power boat away from the yacht, spraying Logan with water and laughing as they sped away. She looked back over her shoulder, and when she was convinced Logan had retreated back to the interior of the yacht, she slowed and took one of the burritos from her.

"Cream and sugar are there," Shiloh said as she picked up the mug that had already been liberally doused with cream.

"She knows how you like yours?" Dallas asked, and Shiloh nodded.

"And will want me to watch how you take yours. Trin is kind of the mother hen of the group. I always feel like I should be because of Mason."

"I like my coffee black. Are they some kind of military unit?"

Shiloh grinned. "SEALs. Mason is technically in command, but that word, when applied to each other, is pretty loose."

Dallas smiled back, relaxed and enjoying herself. "But not so much when applied to their women."

"You got it. There is a much stricter application of the rules when it comes to us women."

"How many of us are there?" Dallas asked, intrigued that she found it so easy to accept she was part of the group.

"Five men and you make four of the women. The only unattached man is Nash. You obviously met Trin and have yet to meet Devon. When you do, don't let the *smarter than everyone else in the room JAG lawyer* demeanor fool you. She's a kick in the ass and has the most delightfully deceitful, dirty mind. It's great fun."

"Just like that, I'm part of the group?" It seemed unbelievable.

"If Logan brought you to the boat, that's good enough for the rest of us. He's a great guy, by the way."

Dallas sighed and felt as if she had truly found a new friend. "I know. Should I be worried about that?"

Shiloh shook her head. "Not in the least. They're all Doms but in the best sense of that word. Yes, they enjoy all the goodies that go along with it, but they don't shirk their responsibilities in that area." She reached out and touched Dallas' arm. "But if it isn't what you want, just say the word."

Dallas said nothing but turned toward the horizon, where she could barely make out the faintest outline of the rig. She needed to get her mind off Logan and all the deliciously wicked things she sensed he could provide and focus on the problem at hand—how to stop the leak, how to clean up the spill, and how had it happened in the first place.

CHAPTER 11

Logan

Logan watched as the boat with Shiloh and Dallas sped away back toward the oil rig. He didn't like the idea of her being on board that rig with all those men. He wasn't worried about her so much as the idea of what all those other men must be thinking when they saw her. He'd need to take her into town and be seen with her. Better yet, put a collar around her neck—something to show she was off-limits, and anyone found tampering with what was his would face serious consequences.

As he headed for the salon, he shook his head. At some point, he was going to have to make amends with Mason, Zak, and Flynn. He'd given them such a raft of shit when they'd fallen as fast and as hard as they had for Shiloh, Trinity and Devon. He hadn't known Dallas for even twenty-four hours, and there he was, staking out his so-called territory.

Jesus, he was as bad as the others... well, except for Nash. But then the rest of them were all agreed that the Bull Shark had succumbed to the sweet siren's song of love a long time ago. Unless they were mistaken, the notoriously moody Bull Shark had a serious thing for one of the doctors based in the secret shark city, El Jardin Secreto.

They all agreed it wasn't a matter of *if* Nash had fallen for Dr. Sydney Walsh, it was only a matter of *when* he acted on those feelings. Given Nash's proclivity for just taking what he wanted, they might need to do some damage control.

Wandering into the salon, he noticed Trinity was sitting comfortably in Zak's lap. Logan wondered if she ever sat anywhere else anymore. Devon was standing and looking through a file with Flynn seated by her side. Mason and Nash were sitting on the other side of the conference table, but Logan noticed Mason had left space for Shiloh to join him.

"It's been an interesting twelve hours." Devon glanced at Logan. "More interesting for some than others."

"That's enough, Dev," Flynn muttered.

She grinned down at him, clearly not taking the reprimand all that seriously. Logan shrugged as he took his seat at the other end of the table, wishing like hell Dallas could be part of this impromptu meeting.

That was a problem and another thing he needed to apologize to his friends for. He'd thought Mason, Zak, and Flynn had jumped the gun in telling the women in their lives about their mutation as soon into the relationship as they had. Now, he wanted to do the same.

Flynn had described it as almost a compulsion to share everything with Devon and how he'd felt as if a weight had been lifted once she knew. The Oceanic Whitetip had shared that there had been a niggling fear that she might reject him once she knew about his hybrid status. Logan shook his head internally; he knew exactly how Flynn felt. He wanted to share all of it—the Kraken, the mutation, everything—with Dallas. Somehow, he knew that he could.

"So, my aide, Carlson, has come up with some interesting information," said Devon. "For instance, our old friend, Eli Green, has reared his ugly head. I think we all agreed from the get-go that Green killed Schumacher. The question was, why? The obvious answer was because Schumacher had outlived his usefulness."

"But what was Green using Schumacher for?" Nash asked.

"The simple answer is the unit. He wanted a demonstration of what you guys could do," answered Devon.

Mason's brow furrowed. "Why? It's not like he can sell us off or even rent us out."

Devon looked at Flynn, who nodded as he spoke. "Tell them."

Devon took a deep breath. "No, but he can sell the ability for someone to create their own."

Nash shook his head. "They're years away from getting the gene mutation therapy to work."

"Devon's discovered hard evidence that they are looking at other ways to create shifters," said Flynn, letting his words sink in.

"Like what?" Nash's brow rose. "They've abandoned the artificial insemination method. It was completely unreliable."

Devon and Flynn were silent.

"Oh shit," Logan sat back, stunned.

Flynn nodded. "They've buried the research and the funding, but some of our medical records have been copied to that portion of the project."

"Care to fill the rest of us in?" asked Zak, who looked up to see the color drain from Trinity's face. "What?"

Devon took a deep breath. "A breeding program."

"I told you, they've abandoned AI," Nash growled.

"Yes, they have," Flynn replied. "Devon found evidence that they tried some things in utero, but they failed as well."

"Christ," swore Mason. "You can't breed a shark to a human."

"No," said Devon softly. "But you can breed a shark-shifter to a human female."

"That's monstrous," whispered Trinity as Zak wrapped his arms more tightly around her.

"They're going to breed super sailors," confirmed Flynn.

"That's not the only dirty little secret we uncovered," continued Devon. "The Admiral's murder wasn't random at all. He'd come across the trail that led us to the super sailor breeding program."

"That's why they killed him," said Logan. "That's got Green's fingerprints all over it. Take out the Admiral and show what we can do at the same time. But who were the guys we killed?"

"Please tell me they weren't US troops?" Mason blew out a breath.

"No," Flynn answered. "We think he's got an interested buyer who had people he wanted eliminated. They set them up to be killed by us. What better demonstration could some megalomaniacal warlord have than that?"

Devon nodded. "Carlson was able to get some files on Green. Carlson is spooked, and as good as he is with a computer, he's out of his depth."

"We need to get to him," Logan rose to his full height.

"Already handled," Devon assured him. "I have some friends who can keep him safe. They confirmed they had him just as we were arriving. As careful as we've been, our knowing the totality or at least most of the moving parts of what Green is up to is bound to get back to him. It'll have him targeting us."

"But what about the men I saw?" asked Trinity.

"We think the guy helping Barry Driscoll was Eli Green. We have yet to figure out what they were loading on the boat, but whatever it is, you can bet Green didn't want it found on the yacht." Devon clarified.

"We think Driscoll is up to his ears in it but hasn't a clue. Our guess is that Green is using *Oceanic Adventures* to transport something—drugs, guns, whatever. He'll keep Driscoll around until he doesn't need him, or he'll set him up to take the fall."

Looking at Logan, Flynn went on, "I had Devon run background on your girl…"

"You what?" snarled Logan.

"Simmer down, Logan. You'd have done the same," Mason interjected. "We've run deep background checks on Shiloh, Trinity, and Devon herself, and Devon is a JAG lawyer. Given the enormity and secrecy of who and what we are, I think the girls understand our need to know precisely who we're dealing with."

Both Trinity and Devon nodded.

"It only makes sense." Trinity soothed.

"Maybe, but I only met the girl last night," groused Logan. "You might have asked."

Devon smiled. "My personal experience is you

boys don't let any grass grow under your feet. Once you have a target in your sights, it's full speed ahead. Any girl shows up here on *Top Secret*, it's a good thing to have a deep background check."

"I suppose you're right. You didn't find anything. I know you didn't," asserted Logan as he realized he was quite certain of that.

"Nothing that our little family would be worried about, but she's an interesting girl—she works for Pistris Oil."

"So?" Logan prickled. "I knew she worked for an oil company. She's their chief environmental cleanup person."

"Did you know Pistris is Latin for shark?" Devon asked. "Care to venture a guess as to who the major shareholder is in Pistris Oil?"

"Green?" Logan's eyebrow arched. When Devon nodded, he pushed back from the table. "As soon as Shiloh gets back, I'm going after her. She can send her resignation from her hotel in La Paz when I check her out. She'll be on board with me."

"Not so quick," Devon countered. "It might be in our interests to have her onboard that rig. It's awfully close to where the Admiral was assassinated—easily close enough to remove something from the yacht to the rig."

"You are **not** sending my woman on a spy mission."

"Not by herself," Mason agreed. "But she knows

the rig. She could take us back there when it was closed down for the night."

"They pump oil twenty-four hours a day, three-hundred-sixty-five." Logan folded his arms across his chest.

"But they're going to have to shut down the pump to deal with the spill, then they'll probably do two eight-hour shifts to work on the cleanup, but that means there are eight hours at night, they'll be shut down, and workers will be in their quarters," Mason explained.

"They'll have proximity alarms," Nash warned.

"For boats." Zak smiled. "Last time I checked, none of us needed a boat to cut through the water." He squeezed Trinity. "And you, Shiloh, and Devon can hold down the fort here."

"No way," snapped Devon. "I can understand Trinity and Shiloh, but I'm Navy, same as you, and if something goes sideways, it might not hurt to have your lawyer handy."

"We can move *Top Secret* closer," Flynn suggested, "and you can stay on board with the rest of the girls as backup. We'll need to make sure Dallas is safe. The fewer non-shifters we have to worry about while we're snooping around on the rig and beneath it, the better. Someone will need to stay here with the girls."

"Short straw," said Nash.

The men all nodded. Before Devon and Trinity could protest further, Shiloh joined them in the salon.

"I like your girl, Logan… oh dear, those aren't happy faces," she said, looking around the room.

"No, baby, they're not," Mason replied. "I'm going to over-ride the short straw. Nash, you need to patrol the Kraken. If it looks quiet, maybe slip into the base and poke around. They're more used to seeing you there. If you can, find a reason to talk to Dr. Walsh. See if you can feel her out for what she knows and if we might be able to count on her."

"I'm not going to ask Logan to stay behind. It's his girl, and he'd never do it. Next to Nash, Zak and I are the biggest. That means Flynn, you're on guard duty—and before I get a lot of flak from anyone, keep in mind, last time I checked, we were a military unit, and I was in command. Besides, Flynn, you and Devon figured this shit out. We need you to keep digging. Try to get a line on Driscoll. He's still something of an unknown. Trinity can help you with that. If he's as clueless as we think, we may have to get him to safety as well. Questions?"

When no one said a word, Mason sighed. "Good. Logan, what time are you picking up your girl?"

"Seven or earlier if she texts me."

Mason nodded. "We'll brief her when she gets here. I don't want her to act suspicious."

Logan turned to him. "It never occurred to you that this might just be a one-night stand?"

Everyone in the room laughed. Logan could feel the heat staining his cheeks.

"Me neither," he said sheepishly.

The meeting over, Logan went outside to get some air. He meant to keep Dallas' involvement to a minimum. She hadn't had a lot of sleep the night before and would be working all day. He waited for Flynn on deck.

"So," started his friend, "the mighty have fallen."

"Man, I never thought…"

"None of us did. Falling for Devon was the easiest, scariest thing I've ever done. But I think your Dallas is going to fit right in, although the idea of she and Devon becoming buddies is daunting."

Logan grinned. "All the more reasons we can spank their pretty little backsides."

Nothing more was said; nothing more needed to be said. Logan and Flynn turned and stared at the horizon, just beyond which was the oil rig on which Dallas was working and that they believed might well hold answers to a lot of questions they had.

CHAPTER 12

Eli Green

Staring out at the crystal blue waters of the ocean, Green turned his face to the sun. Yesterday had been an excellent day, and he had no doubt that today would prove to be even better. Every day was a holiday when you were the boss.

"Mr. Green?"

Green turned at Andre's voice to find his head of security waiting at the edge of the enormous pool. It was never enough to have the sea at hand for Green. He always expected a private pool to play in as well. It was one of the many advantages of owning multiple properties in just about every time zone.

"What is it, Andre?"

"I just wanted to check in with you about today." Andre strode around the side of the pool.

"Go on." Green had always liked Andre. Cool,

calm and efficient, Andre was also a wall of solid muscle who was useful with a weapon.

"We're heading to Pistris Oil?"

"That's right." Green's lips curled. It had been too long since he'd paid Zander Effron a visit. It was time to check in and see how his latest transaction was doing.

"Any other plans, Sir?"

"No." Green had already decided. Today was a day for playing. "Pablo is bringing some women back here later, so I expect they'll keep me busy for an hour or two."

Andre's laughter danced around the water, and Green joined the sentiment. "Sounds like a good plan, Sir. Shall I ask Saul to bring the car around?"

"Yes," Green nodded before Andre stalked away, knowing his driver, Saul, would already be waiting. His staff, like everything in Green's world, were discreet, professional, and reliable. They never questioned an order and never made him wait. That was just how he liked it.

Turning back to the ocean, he breathed in the unmistakable scent of sea air. The sooner he dealt with the oil company, the sooner he could have some fun.

∽

Less than half an hour later, he arrived at Pistris Oil. Green straightened his lapels as he exited his car and made his way into the glass-fronted lobby area. Naturally, the people there knew who he was, and he was ushered up to the very top of the building, where a bronzed-looking Zander was waiting.

"Green." Zander extended him a hand, his polished performance almost as dazzling as his dental work. "Good to see you."

"Likewise." Green shook his hand, allowing Zander to steer him to his office.

"Coffee?" Zander glanced back. "Or something stronger?"

"Coffee is good," Green replied. As far as he knew, there were few reasons to celebrate their collaboration yet. He'd been a major shareholder at Pistris Oil since Zander was in prep school, enjoying the benefits of the company's success, but it was their most recent involvement that he'd come to discuss. Green needed safe transit for his product, but perhaps more importantly, he wanted to know who he could trust.

"Helena." Zander clicked his fingers at the young blonde sitting behind the desk outside his office. "Bring us coffee."

"Yes, Mr. Effron," she answered, rising from her chair to comply.

Green's gaze lingered over her backside as she

scurried away. He could certainly see why Zander had chosen her for the role.

"After you." Zander opened the door to his huge ocean view office, gesturing for Green to go inside.

"Thanks."

He wandered into the space, impressed by the sleek modern design. Zander might not have his father's business experience, but he had good taste, and based on everything Green had garnered, he had the right approach to succeed.

"So, what brings you here?" Zander's tone was casual, but the way he held himself as he strode to his desk suggested to Green that he already knew the answer. "Not that it's not lovely to have you, of course."

"I want to talk about our deal." Green opted to get straight to the point as he sunk into the chair opposite Zander's desk. He had little time or patience to dance around it. "How is it progressing?"

"The *latest* deal?" Zander's brow rose as he sat down.

"That's right." Irritation spiked at Zander's delay. Surely, he knew which deal Green was referring to?

"It's all good." Zander's voice was a little too enthusiastic. "Everything is on track."

"Really?" Green's eyebrow arched. "Because I heard about the slick, and I wouldn't want any of my *merchandise* to get mixed up in that problem.

"Of course not." Zander laughed, although something about the sound was brittle. "Your barrels were not affected."

"You're sure?"

"One hundred percent." Zander grinned, revealing a row of perfect teeth. "The deal and your barrels are intact."

"That's good." Green had hoped to feel more reassured, but something about Zander's demeanor troubled him. Perhaps it was just his age and comparative inexperience? Green couldn't quite put his finger on it, but he never ignored his gut instinct. "Because I have additional barrels that need disposal, and I'm counting on you."

Naturally, that wasn't true. Green had numerous contacts he could negotiate with to permanently discard his materials, but he'd decided to use this as a test. If he gave Zander more responsibility, and he came through, then Green would know he could be trusted. If, on the other hand, Zander chose to let Green down, then Green would have learned something about the man. He'd manage that situation as well. As the majority shareholder at Pistris, Green would be happy to take the reins if the CEO suddenly disappeared on a permanent sabbatical.

"Well, we're happy to help." Zander pressed his elbows into the black desk.

Green was betting he was. Not only was their deal easy business for Pistris Oil, but it was lucrative too, and keeping it all below the gaze of the authorities meant there was no need for tax avoidance.

A soft knock at the door jarred Green's attention from Zander's conceited smile, and turning, he noticed the petite blonde entering with a tray of refreshments.

"Ah, Helena." Zander's smile widened as she brought the tray over to a nearby table. "Lovely."

As she bent over the surface to prepare the coffee, Green had to agree; she was lovely. He hoped Pablo would bring something as enticing to his pool party later.

"How do you like your coffee, Mr. Green?" Helena asked.

So, she knew who he was then? That was pleasing. Maybe he'd invite her along and discover how that perfect shade of lipstick looked around his cock.

"Just a little milk," he answered, enjoying the view as she swiveled to comply. "I'm very specific about what I like."

She peered over her shoulder, a gorgeous blush growing on her cheeks. Glancing up, Green followed Zander's gaze back to Helena and wondered if he'd already had the pleasure. That wasn't an attractive prospect, the idea polluting his fantasy.

"Thank you, Helena." Zander smirked as she placed the cups down. "You may leave us."

"Yes, Mr. Effron." Her tone was understandably

nervous as she tottered away and closed the door behind her.

"Nice assistant." Reaching for his coffee, Green breathed in the rich aroma.

"You don't have one?" Zander sounded amused at the notion.

"I only hire men." Green didn't know why he felt the need to explain himself to the younger man, but the words were out of his mouth before he'd had time to consider them. "They're more dependable and infinitely stronger."

"But not as pretty." Zander chuckled.

"No." Green couldn't argue with that. "But fortunately, I have ways to deal with that problem as well." His lips twitched, imagining the bevy of beauties Pablo would bring back for him later. "So, about the slick…" He paused, paying attention to Zander's face. "Is it something we need to worry about?" Not that Green gave a damn about the marine environment, but it wasn't the best publicity in this day and age.

"It's being dealt with." Zander waved his hand dismissively. "I have my people on it."

"Your best men?" Green pressed. "I'm sure we both agree we don't want any reason for groups like Greenpeace to show up."

Zander laughed, the insidious sound one of the few things Green liked about him. "Woman, actually."

"You chose a woman to manage this?" Green's brow furrowed.

"She's the best there is. She has an outstanding reputation and puts a pretty face on it." Zander smiled. "They can be useful for things other than sex, Green."

"That's not my experience," Green muttered, though it was true he'd probably never given them a chance. "But okay, you run this show." He gestured around the office. "Just make sure it doesn't affect the share price."

"It won't."

Green didn't much care for the expression on Zander's face, the one that inferred he was too old and out of touch to understand how the world worked.

"Anything else I can help with?" Green offered.

He didn't especially want to aid the smug little prick sitting opposite him, but he knew it was better to keep allies close and enemies even closer. Zander's father was still a liability, and his son was fast becoming the same. Lips curling, Green remembered he didn't have allies nor many remaining enemies, but he would do what he had to do.

"No, thank you." Zander looked stunned, as well he might. "But I'll give you a call if I think of anything."

Green smiled, sipping his coffee. He made a mental note to ignore any incoming calls from Effron.

He didn't want to speak to the asshole again until he knew he could be trusted.

He'd even been known to help out the little people when it was required. His mind recollected a night not so long before when he'd helped the tedious Driscoll smuggle barrels of his product away from a posh event. Driscoll had thought himself clever in secreting it aboard the yacht while the Admiral would be onboard, meaning they wouldn't be subject to random searches. What Driscoll hadn't known was that Green had planned a demonstration of the Guardian Project's prowess for that same evening. The Admiral had become a problem. He was a man of integrity and honor with serious political aspirations and delusions of grandeur.

Green had planned to kill two birds with one stone—literally. He'd neutralize the Admiral while at the same time put on a practical demonstration of what his super soldiers could do. The warlord who had the most money and interest in acquiring that particular product had people he wanted to eliminate, so he had sent them on a bogus mission to kill the Admiral. Green had known with the Admiral dead, the Guardian Project's protective detail would go into action to neutralize the threat.

The plan would have been a smashing success except for the fact that Driscoll—the cheap bastard—had planned to use the yacht to transport some of the barrels for delivery to the Pistris oil rig for disposal.

Green had been caught between a rock and a hard place when he realized that barrels of the toxic waste were on board. It would have been a problem if they had been found when the authorities swept the super yacht. So, he and Driscoll had acted and had removed the waste to a smaller power boat to be transported to the rig. Men like Driscoll were useful puppets to keep dangling and usually managed to hang themselves. Besides, he might need Driscoll as a sacrificial lamb to drop through the trapdoor of the gallows if that pesky JAG lawyer got too close. He smiled as the plan formed in his head.

CHAPTER 13

Dallas

Dallas allowed the wind blowing in her hair and the coffee to do their jobs. She was finally able to shake some of the sexual thrall she'd felt in Logan's presence.

"It'll come right back." Shiloh chuckled as she steered the boat on a direct course for the rig.

Dallas turned and looked at Shiloh with confusion. "What'll come right back?"

Shiloh laughed harder. "All those delicious, wicked feelings you get from Logan. It can be abated if they aren't right there, but the second they put their hand on you and breathe in your scent, it's all over."

"I'm not sure what you're talking about. I mean, I had a great time with Logan. He's amazing…"

"Oh man, you've got it bad." Shiloh smiled. "I remember thinking that. It's just a one-night stand.

He couldn't have been that great. Did I really let him do that to me? Did I really get that turned on?"

"You misunderstand. The D/s stuff I totally get. I've been going to clubs for years."

Shiloh throttled back and turned to look at Dallas, taking a sip of her own coffee. "You've been going to clubs and *playing*, and therein lies the difference. These guys don't play. They live and believe in the lifestyle as a way of life. I'd never been exposed to it before I got together with Mason. I'd read a couple of books I never wanted people to find on my Kindle but never experienced it."

She shook her head with a rueful grin. "You think it's hard for you? At least you understand it and have accepted that part of yourself that needs to submit to a dominant man. But me? Oh, hell no. I put Mason through so much shit, I still feel guilty. Only difference is now, when he senses it, he just spanks me until I'm over it."

Dallas grinned. "Isn't it awful that having some man blister your ass can do so much good for you?"

Shiloh restarted the engine. "Devon says for her, it stops the hamster wheel in her head."

"I know just what she means, but it doesn't mean that it's Logan specific."

"Oh yes, it does. Trust me, you will never find a more possessive, territorial group of men in your life. But each one of them would die for his woman, for his brothers-in-arms, and for that guy's woman as well. They have a protocol in place that if it all goes to hell, their women get protected first. They might be willing to sacrifice themselves for their country, but never their women."

"You love him… Mason, I mean."

Shiloh nodded. "I do. The lot of them all crack me up. They've convinced themselves they're invincible and that they need sex, but not love. They couldn't be more wrong. I will give them this, once they've found their woman, they are all in, and nothing will stop them."

"You don't know that Logan feels that way about me."

"Sure, I do. You were on *Top Secret*. They don't bring casual visitors to the ship, ever. And he's planning to come get you tonight and let me guess, wants you to text him when I drop you off."

"He's a controlling sonofabitch." Dallas couldn't resist her smile.

"No, he's a *caring* one. They aren't much better when we're in the U.S., but here, especially in the Sea of Cortez and in this part of the Pacific, there are pirates, drug runners, arms dealers, and the like. Not exactly safe."

Dallas sagged against the seat back. "So, feeling this connection is normal?"

"Yes. Annoying but normal. But hey, look on the bright side—you get amazing sex and three new girlfriends."

Dallas laughed out loud. "What more could a girl ask for?"

"Seriously, Dallas, if you don't think you can be happy…"

"That's the scary part. I don't know that I could ever be happy without him again."

"Don't worry. The scary part passes pretty quickly."

"I just don't know how it can work with my job. I mean, I go all over the world."

"Logan has responsibilities as well," Shiloh replied. "But ask yourself which you'd rather do without."

"You may have a point. They're stationed out of San Diego?"

"Coronado mostly. Trinity and Zak have a beach cottage there. In fact, I used to own it. Currently, Mason and I live either on my boat, which I had visions of sailing around the world in, or aboard *Top Secret*. He prefers to be on *Top Secret* as it has a biometric alarm system and so is pretty safe. The safer Logan knows you are, the easier it will be for him to be on patrol."

The rig was now in sight.

"Do you think I'm an idiot?" Dallas asked.

"No. I think you're a woman who got steamrolled by a super sexy hunk and isn't sure what comes next." Shiloh smiled.

"Care to clue me in?"

"No way. I will tell you that whatever comes up, just hold tight to Logan and the fact that he loves you…"

"Whoa. Nobody has said a word about love," Dallas interrupted her.

"He does, and he will tell you. Keep in mind things are moving just as fast for him. Like the others, he never expected it to happen. But I know Logan. He's all in. He'll never let you down. It's not in his DNA."

Shiloh expertly sidled the boat up to the rig so Dallas could step out.

"Thanks for the ride."

"Don't forget to text Logan." Shiloh's grin widened.

Dallas stood looking at her phone as Shiloh pulled away. She grinned as she realized the redhead hadn't tried to douse her with spray for the speedboat. Now, how to start the text? Logan? Babe? Sweetheart? Master? No, way too soon for Master or pet names.

Logan,
It's Dallas Miles.
Shiloh dropped me at the rig.
I hope I see you tonight.
Dallas

The minute she hit send, she felt stupid. Dallas Miles, well, duh. How many other people named Dallas did he know? Not a lot. Then she signed off with a wimpy 'I hope…' and signed her name. God, she was an idiot. She hadn't even made the ladder to climb up from the docking station to the main platform of the rig when her cell vibrated.

I knew it was you, Baby.
Good girl for letting me know.
We'll discuss you not being
certain about tonight. I
will pick you up at seven
if not before.
If you can get away before
then, text or call me and
I'll come and get you.
Logan

Dallas was beaming as she stepped up onto the main platform of the rig. Her smile faded as she realized that once again, nothing was being done. Men were just standing around, and the only sound she could hear was the rhythmic sound of the pump, spilling more crude oil into the ocean's fragile ecosystem.

She might be Logan's *baby*, but she was the boss of this mess and this crew. "You," she said, pointing to one of the workers. "Get a boat ready to take me out. I want to survey the damage and what, if anything, has been done."

"But the boss said…"

Dallas stepped into the man's personal space. "Listen up. Until this spill is cleaned up, *I am* the boss. The only guy that has more authority than me is Zander Effron. You do know who that is, right? He's the guy that signs your paycheck, but only if I tell him that you're doing your job. Now get me a boat."

"Yes, ma'am."

She grabbed his sleeve as he started to leave. "Where's Barney?"

"Up in the wheelhouse."

The instant she let go, he scurried away, as did all the others who'd been in the vicinity. Well, at least they'd established who was alpha on the rig. 'Wheelhouse' was something of a misnomer as it generally referred to the part of a boat or ship where steering and speed were controlled. On a rig this big, it was stationary and had no steering or way to move it without it being disassembled and towed away. But the name for the office stuck.

Dallas climbed the ladder to the wheelhouse, stood on the landing for a moment to gather herself, and stepped inside. She wasn't sure who the guy in the suit was, but it didn't matter. She had an oil spill to clean up. And the first step in doing that was to stop the goddamn pump.

"Barney," she bellowed from across the room. "What the hell are you doing here?"

To his credit, Barney jumped and swung around, donut in his mouth for only a second before he spat it out.

"Miss Miles."

Time to show him how she'd earned her reputation as the alpha bitch of Pistris Oil.

"I know I wasn't here at o'dawn thirty this morning. I guess I supposed a man with your experience and pay grade would make damn sure by the time I got here, work was underway."

"I was just getting started when Mr. Green came on board and told me to stand down."

Dallas whirled around to face the stranger, noting his fine linen suit and the helicopter up on the platform. "Just who do you think you are to be giving orders to my men?" she challenged.

She was fairly sure she saw him inhale deeply and smile as he recognized the lingering aroma of sex. To a man who had certain proclivities and was observant, it was probably fairly easy to notice. He might not know who the man was, but he'd be able to tell she'd just left some guy's bed. As Logan had predicted, she'd been dripping his cum onto the seam of her jeans since she'd pulled them on.

"As Barney here told you, I'm Eli Green, a major shareholder in Pistris Oil. The man you fired yesterday works for my company."

If he thought she was going to be impressed by his helicopter, fancy manner, fine suit, and manicured hands, he had another thought coming. The difference between his hands and Logan's was Logan's were calloused, had more strength, and knew a lot of ways to bring pleasure to his woman. *His woman.* She found she rather liked the sound of that.

"That's kind of a conflict of interest, isn't it, Mr. Green? *Pistris Oil* hires a major shareholder's company to clean up a spill, and I find he and Barney here schmoozing it up with donuts and coffee when I arrive, the pump still leaking oil into the ocean and not a goddamn thing being done to fix the problem. Do the other shareholders know about you and Effron's cozy little arrangement?"

Green had an outstanding poker face. His eyes only widened infinitesimally as his pupils dilated. He wasn't used to being challenged, especially, she bet, by a woman.

"I don't believe there is a conflict, especially given my company's bid was the lowest," Green said, barely managing to keep his tone civil. "Barney was waiting for Pete to arrive."

"I've played that game with your kind before. You estimate 'X' many days to clean up the spill at a certain cost per day, then somehow, the cleanup takes far longer than you thought it would. Tell me, do you kick back any of the excess profit to anyone at Pistris? As for Pete, I kicked his ass off my rig yesterday. I can do it again today."

She pulled out her cell phone, texted a message and sent it.

Green had a smirky look on his face. Dallas

wondered if he knew how stupid it looked on a man of his age.

"Texting Zander?" he asked smarmily.

"Zander Effron? Head of the company? Nope. Just wanted to let my boyfriend know I had trouble on the rig, and I might be earlier or later than we'd planned. Although texting Zander might not be a bad idea. He can either back me and order you and your flunky to stay the fuck away from my rig, or he can fire me. In which case, my next phone call is to the press about how the company knows it has a leak, knows the pump is still functioning and spilling oil, and is doing nothing about it including," she turned to Barney as she went on, "shutting the fucking pump off."

"Your boyfriend?" Green's brow rose. "You have to call your boyfriend for backup? Not very feministic of you."

"Trust me, Green, my feminism does not require your approval and has Logan's full support…"

The color drained from Green's face. "Logan Knight?"

"Yeah, the SEAL. Heard of him? I assure you Pete has, and Petey boy isn't going to want any part of me or my boyfriend."

Green snatched her phone away, and his face became a pale version of his name.

Logan,
May be earlier or later

*than expected. Some asshole
named Green is here
and is prohibiting cleanup.
Apparently, he's Pete from
the bar's boss.
Fun times.
Dallas*

CHAPTER 14

Logan

Anger surged through Logan's body, merging with his adrenaline as he re-read Dallas' message. "He's on the rig." Logan was on his feet in a heartbeat, charging for the salon door.

"Wait, who's on the rig?" Mason glanced up from his paperwork, his brow creasing as the attention of everyone assembled turned to Logan.

"That fucker, Green." Logan's jaw clenched. "He's on the rig with Dallas."

"What?" Zak straightened beside Trinity.

"I'm taking the power boat." Logan's fury was making it difficult to think. "Fuck that, I'm going to shift and swim over there right now. It's faster."

"Logan, wait." Flynn caught his arm. "Don't do anything reckless. Is Dallas okay?"

Pulling in a deep breath, Logan glanced down at

his phone again. "I think so." He hoped so. "But we all know what Green is like."

"She seemed like she could take care of herself," Trinity reassured him. "And she's the boss on that rig, isn't she? She'll be all right, Logan."

"I still don't like it." Rage throbbed in Logan's head, pounding like a freight train. "I'm going to her."

"I get it." Mason rose and wandered the short distance to where Logan stood. "Any of us would feel the same, but Flynn is right. You need to be careful. If we want to check out the rig later, we don't want to throw all our cards into the air. Green can know you and Dallas are an item, and…" he paused. "You *are* an item, right?"

"Of course." Logan blew out a breath, exasperated. As far as he was concerned, they were. If he had his way, Dallas would never be leaving his side again. Fleetingly, he acknowledged how crazy that sounded after only one night of passion, but he didn't care.

"Good." Mason's lips curled. "So, if you go there, that's the agenda you push with Green, but we don't want to offer him anything else. Turning up as a Mako would be giving him a little too much."

"It sounds like he might already know about us." Nash shook his head from the other side of the room. "Based on what we know, that prick has fingers in a lot of pies."

This time Mason's jaw tightened. "Maybe he does."

Logan could tell it pained Mason to admit it. He knew just how their leader felt. The idea of scum like Green being *in* on their secret was sickening.

"But that doesn't mean we need to go gifting him anything else." Mason's tone was resolved.

"Okay." Logan's head was finally starting to clear, his fingers flying over his device. "I'll take the boat when Shiloh returns. I can go and back Dallas up."

The others continued to talk as he composed a quick message. He had to let Dallas know he was on his way.

Baby,
I'm sure you've figured
this out, but Green is trouble.
I'm coming to make
sure you're okay.
(And no, there's no point
telling me not to bother.
I'm on my way.)
Logan

He would happily have a discussion with her properly about how she *was* his responsibility now and how he wanted to take care of her—but later—when they were together.

"I think that's Shiloh now."

Logan glanced up at Mason's statement, tuning into the noise of the boat from beyond *Top Secret*.

"I'll go and fill her in on what's happening." Mason bolted for the exit, and Logan followed close behind him as his phone vibrated in his hand.

You don't need to come.
I'm fine, honestly.
I'll text when I'm done here.
Dallas
x

His nostrils flared at Dallas' reply. So, she'd added a kiss at the end of her name. No doubt in some vain attempt to placate him, but it wasn't going to work. He was headed her way, and that was final.

"Logan!"

He paused at the sound of Flynn's voice, glancing over his shoulder. "What man? I have to go to her!"

"I know." Flynn's palms rose in a gesture of conciliation. "Just be careful, okay? Green is no bar room thug. He's a nefarious sonofabitch who doesn't play by the rules."

Logan's heart pounded harder at his friend's assessment. "Thanks, I feel loads better that Dallas is there with him."

"I just mean, play the overprotective boyfriend, but don't give him anything else to use against us. He may not know that we even know who he is. The less he knows about us or what we know, the better." Flynn's voice was imploring. "And take care of yourself."

"I'll be fine," Logan insisted, though he knew he'd

feel the same way if Flynn or one of the others was headed out on a similar mission.

Turning back to where Shiloh and Mason were now engaged in conversation, he hurried toward the ramp.

"Logan, Mason just told me about Eli Green." She patted him on the shoulder, but somehow, the more people mentioned Green, the less reassured Logan felt.

"Yeah, I'm going now." He offered them both a small nod as he climbed on board the smaller vessel.

"Call us if you need help." Mason's tone was loaded with the same tension furling in Logan's chest, and peering over his shoulder, Logan offered him a grateful smile.

"I will. Thanks."

∼

The short journey to the rig was agonizing. As the fastest swimmer in the group, the temptation to abandon the boat and just dive into the blue was off the charts, but Logan understood his friend's apprehensions. The last thing a man as dangerous as Green needed was ammunition to use against them.

Dangerous. The word bounced around his head, taunting Logan as the rig came into sight, looming larger as he pushed the boat's engine to its maximum speed. Green was the epitome of the word, and however smart and capable Dallas was, she had no idea of the kind of man she was forced into proximity with. Logan's hand balled into a fist as the thought cemented. Damn the consequences. He didn't care what anyone said, if that jerk so much as laid an idle threat at his woman, Logan would cut Green up so small that the fish wouldn't need to chew.

His lips twitched as he considered his emotive response. He'd only known Dallas for a matter of hours, but he already considered her to be *his woman*. What the hell was this consuming feeling blooming inside him? Could he actually be falling in love with her?

He left the question alone as he pulled up to the rig, securing the boat before climbing onto the docking platform. A couple of guys looked up as he strode past, but any complaints they had seemed to be muted by his sheer determination. No doubt his size and stature helped as well. Approaching a corner of the rig, he caught Dallas' voice on the breeze. Logan paused, glancing around the equipment to catch sight of her.

There she was—his racing heart acknowledged her presence as his ears strained to hear the conversation properly. Dallas was involved in a rather animated conversation with a guy in a suit, and Logan didn't need to be a rocket scientist to figure out who he was. *Green.*

"I already told you, I make the rules on this rig,

Green." Dallas wagged her finger in his direction.

"Actually, the rig belongs to Mr. Effron." Green folded his arms, but it was the amused leer on his face that grated with Logan. He didn't like the thought of any man seeing Dallas as nothing but an attractive annoyance, and if it irritated him, Logan could only imagine how vexed Dallas was. "And he is more than happy for me to be here."

"Then he can tell me that himself." Her hands fell to her hips, one foot tapping against the structure. "He's my boss, not you."

"For the time being."

"What was that?" Dallas advanced on him, and even though she was almost a foot shorter than the man in the expensive suit, Logan noticed the way Green recoiled. Pride bubbled in Logan's chest at the sight. Trinity was right. Dallas could take care of herself—but that didn't mean he wouldn't always be there to help her from now on. "What's that supposed to mean?"

"I'm sure a clever girl like you can figure it out." Green's lips stretched into a sinister smile. "And until then—"

"Dallas." Logan had moved close enough for his voice to carry at regular volume, his introduction halting Green's sentence. "Are you okay?"

Her gaze darted to Logan, and even though he'd

half expected to see indignation at his arrival, he only noticed desire and thankfulness flashing in her beautiful eyes. "I'm okay." Her demeanor softened a little as he approached. Rolling up his sleeves, Logan paced into the fray.

"Mr. Knight, I presume?" Green's eyebrow cocked, despite the color draining from his face.

"That's right. I heard some asshole was bothering Miss Miles." Moving in beside her, he captured her hand in his, reassured as she slid her slender digits between his. "Are you that asshole?"

"I'm Mr. Green." The idiot grinned as if Logan would be impressed by the mention of his name. "Eli Green."

He thrust his palm out in Logan's direction.

"Good for you." Ignoring his offer of a handshake, Logan's stare drilled into Green. "You didn't answer my question. Are you bothering Miss Miles?"

"I'm merely updating her on the latest developments." His greasy hand slunk back to his suit pocket. "There's no reason for concern."

Dallas' gaze flitted to Logan's.

"Is that right?" Logan's voice was softer as he addressed her. "Do I have any reasons to be worried?"

"I'm fine." Her back straightened with the verdict. "But Mr. Green's assessment is untrue."

"Untrue?" Both men queried her logic at the same time.

"Yes." She suppressed the smile that rose. "I'm afraid so."

"How?" Logan encouraged. "What's happened?"

"Misrepresentation." Her brow rose as her attention returned to Green. "Mr. Green is definitely an asshole."

CHAPTER 15

Dallas

Dallas wasn't sure how her pronouncement was going to go over with Logan. She was relieved when he only chuckled quietly.

"He is also trying to make you believe Effron backed whatever play it is he is trying to make." She turned to confront Green. "Effron was very clear that cleaning up the spill is the company's number one priority and responsibility for that rests with me."

"Then I believe you misunderstood, Miss Miles." Green's expression hardened. "He was clear that as a major shareholder, I was to be afforded every courtesy."

"That won't be a problem. I will have someone courteously fish you out of the oil spill after I dropkick your ass off my rig and take you back to the mainland where you are free to file your complaint with Mr. Effron."

Green bristled, and she sensed Logan tensing behind her, ready to spring if he thought she couldn't handle it. Something about his not taking over touched her deeply, and she had to focus on the matter at hand. Dallas watched as Green struggled to maintain his composure, as did others around him.

She was certain some of the men aboard the rig cared about the oil spill, while others, like Barney, would prefer Green's way of doing business—not caring at all about the environment, just as long as they could collect a paycheck. Time to draw a line in the sand and see where those on the rig stood.

Dallas spun to face Barney. "You're fired, too."

"I'm what?" he stammered.

"You heard me. Under your watch, something has gone seriously wrong with this operation, and as far as I can see, you haven't so much as lifted a finger to clean up your mess." She turned to Logan, hoping she hadn't read him wrong. "Babe, can you do me an enormous favor?"

"It would be my pleasure," he purred, turning her insides to goo and wanting nothing more than to find somewhere to screw his brains out.

"We only have one boat at the rig; would you mind taking Barney and Green back to the mainland?"

"What's in it for me?" he teased, clearly enjoying the banter.

"How about a repeat of last night?" She dragged her finger down his torso from the hollow of his throat, stopping right at the top button of his jeans.

Logan chuckled. "Baby, for that, I would lay waste to the world." Dallas leaned in and kissed him, her lips parting and inviting him to slide his tongue inside her mouth to dance and play with hers. "I'm going to hold you to that." He turned to Green and glanced up at Barney. "Gentlemen? I believe the lady asked you to get off her rig. I promise you, my invitation won't be nearly as polite."

"What about my helicopter?" snarled Green.

"Instruct your pilot to fly it off my rig and back to the mainland," said Dallas.

Dallas faced the crowd that had gathered. "Anyone else not wanting to work their asses off to get this spill stopped and then cleaned up should leave with Logan."

Several men stepped forward, and Logan gestured to the docking platform. When Green failed to move, Logan grasped his upper arm. "The lady asked you nicely to leave. I won't be nearly as civilized." He leaned over to kiss Dallas' cheek. "I'll see that they all get back to shore. You go save the ocean, and I'll see you tonight."

"Thanks. I appreciate your help."

Logan chuckled. "It isn't you who should be

thanking me. I saw what you did to Pete last night. I'll get them out of your hair."

Dallas watched as Logan easily strong-armed Green off the rig, admiring the way his ass filled out his jeans.

"Sigh. That is one good-looking hunk of a man," one of the female roughnecks said.

"He is indeed. Now, let's get to work."

"You heard the boss lady," one of the other workers clapped his hands together.

Even though she had lost about a quarter of the crew who'd walked off with Barney and Green, Dallas was pleased not only with the rest of their hard work but with their commitment to getting the spill cleaned up. Shutting down the pump had proved more difficult than she'd imagined.

It should have been relatively easy and safe to do so. It was almost as if someone or something was working against them. In the end, they were able to isolate the problem shutting the pump down, but they would still need to figure out what had caused it to malfunction and fix it.

Because of Barney's incompetence, laziness, or sabotage, the spill had spread too far for the oil booms to be of any real effect. They had slowed the spread but hadn't stopped it.

"Let's get the skimmers started on the area we were able to contain." Dallas looked through the rig's manifest of what was on board.

"What about the part we didn't get to fast enough?" The worker's face was pale. "Shit. We should have done something. We just let Barney tell us to keep on with our other work."

"You didn't know," Dallas said consolingly. "But it's good to know Barney actively told you to stand down. Can you direct the skimmers?"

"Yes, ma'am."

"Good. I'm putting you in charge of that. I'll start trying to come up with a plan to deal with the rest."

"We're on it, boss."

Dallas smiled as he left her and started gathering the crew that would start removing the oil. As Dallas saw it, she had two major issues: the first was to contain and mitigate the damage of the spill itself; the second was to figure out what had gone wrong and fix it.

Her cell phone vibrated, and she reached into her pocket to get it, grinning as she did so, thinking it would be Logan. It wasn't. Her smile faded as her caller ID identified the caller—Mitchell Effron—Zander's father, who was retired but still the Board Chairman. Best to take a polite, professional, respectful tone.

"Dallas Miles."

"Dallas, it's Mitch."

Referring to himself as Mitch in a friendly voice was a good sign.

"Mitch. What can I do for you?" she asked civilly.

It had been Mitchell Effron who had convinced her to come to work for Pistris.

"I'm not sure what you did, but whatever it was had my son and my largest shareholder spitting nails and calling you all kinds of nasty things in a video conference."

I'll bet. "Sorry about having to toss Green off the rig. He was causing problems, and honestly, it isn't safe for a greenhorn to be out here right now."

Mitch chuckled. "I say this with nothing but respect, Dallas. You've got a set of balls on you I wish I had. I don't think I've ever heard Green quite that angry. Why don't you catch me up?"

"We've contained the majority of the spill with booms, and the remainder of the crew is starting in with the skimmers. The problem is Barney actually ordered the guys to stand down, so we didn't get started soon enough, and the asshole wouldn't turn the pump off."

"Do you know what went wrong?"

"Not yet," she answered honestly. "We had trouble shutting down the pump but managed it. I want to focus on cleaning up the spill and mitigating the damage that's been done. Then I'll focus on figuring out what went wrong and fixing it."

"Sounds like you've got it under control. Do you need me to have Zander send more men?"

"I think at this point, we're best to go with the crew we have. They're working well together. I think adding more men would be a distraction, and we'd lose time trying to get them up-to-speed."

"Fine," Mitch replied. "I'll leave it in your hands. I hope you know I have every confidence in your ability to manage this thing. As you might imagine, our media people are having a meltdown. I may need you to come in, look pretty and smile for the cameras."

Dallas smiled. One of the things she'd always liked about Mitchell Effron was, for a businessman, he seemed to care deeply for the environment.

"I can do that. I'll need a couple of hours to get cleaned up. Right now, I don't think there's a single inch of my body that isn't grimy."

"My guess is that man of yours would be happy to help get you cleaned up. If you think Green was pissed at you, trust me, it was nothing compared to what he had to say about your boyfriend. Green seems to think he's a SEAL. Do you think they'll give us trouble?"

"Logan cares deeply about the environment," she explained. "It's one of the things we have in common. I think he, and probably his unit, will help in whatever way they can. If you're worried about the Navy or the Coast Guard, these aren't U.S. territorial waters, so they have no jurisdiction and aren't on overly friendly terms with the Mexican authorities."

"What about the Mexicans?"

"We haven't seen them at all, which is a bit

surprising. I'd have thought they would have been all over this, but according to our people here on the rig, there's been no sign of them. It might be prudent to reach out to them proactively. I can do that by phone, but it would be problematic for me to leave the rig to take a day to do that."

"I tell you what, you write me a sit rep, and I'll reach out to my contacts in the government down there. I'll take one of the private jets down and meet with them and see if I can't buy us a little grace. Any chance you could do a small press conference the day after tomorrow?"

"Sure thing. It might take me that long to get cleaned up," she said with a laugh.

"I doubt that. Maybe you and your man can have breakfast with me before we go face the sharks."

"I'm not sure what time commitments Logan has, but I can make myself available, and I will most definitely invite him."

"Good. At least now I'll be guaranteed at least one friendly face."

"No worries on that account." She smiled. "I'll get you that report before I leave the rig."

"Thanks, Dallas. I'll see you the day after tomorrow."

"I look forward to it."

That had gone a whole lot better than she thought it would. Dallas glanced at her watch and texted Logan:

Going to be a little later than 7.
Spoke to the Chairman of the Board and need to
get him a sit rep before I'm
free for the evening.
Late date?
Dallas

The reply was almost instantaneous:
You don't get off that easy.
I don't want you on the rig after
dark. I'll bring dinner and sit quietly
while you finish your report.
Then we'll head for home.
I had fun today. Green and
Barney were pissed.
Logan

Dallas shook her head and turned her attention back to her most pressing issues so that she'd be in a position to get her report done as soon as possible. She continued to comb through the maintenance records and Barney's required daily logs. The maintenance looked to have been kind of hit and miss, but Barney's logs were enlightening, not so much in what they said but their condition. It was obvious that not only had they been altered, but in a couple of places, it appeared someone else had written them—not only in the language used but in the handwriting itself.

CHAPTER 16

Logan

Logan arrived back on the rig just as the sun was setting on the horizon. At this time of the day, the urge to dive into the deep tugged inside, and he was thankful that he'd had the foresight to cool off in the blue before he'd reached the isolated place.

"Hey, handsome." Dallas offered him a furtive wave as she stepped toward him. The last fragments of the day slipped away behind her. "Thanks for offering to keep me safe. I'm not used to playing the damsel in distress, but I have to admit, I was grateful to have you around earlier."

He sensed there was more she wanted to say but noticed the way her lips pressed together.

"You're welcome." Logan placed down the basket of snacks Flynn and Devon had helped him cobble together, taking her in his arms. "I'm always going to keep you safe."

Pressing his lips to hers, they shared a slow, sensual kiss—the kind that stirred his fervor. He fisted her hair, relishing her groan as he contemplated just dropping down on the rig and going for it, but no—a woman like Dallas deserved better than some dirty work fuck. She deserved the world.

"I mean it," he whispered into the side of her neck. "I'm here for you—whatever you need."

Fleetingly, Logan acknowledged it was a bold claim to make to a woman he'd only spent one night with, but yet again, he had the sense that nothing had ever been more right. He *did* want to take care of Dallas. There was something about her that called to a part of his soul in a way scarily reminiscent of the draw of the Kracken. He didn't want to lose this feeling.

Tilting her chin in his direction, he stroked the side of her face as he went on. "How have you been getting on here? The spill looks more contained than earlier."

"Yeah." She sighed, demonstrating how much effort had gone into the cleanup so far. "Now the deadwood's been removed, we're making progress, but I am hungry."

"For what, baby?" He could hardly resist teasing her.

"For you *and* whatever you've brought in your

basket, Sir." Her lips stretched into a gorgeous smile, reminding him of the temptress who'd taken his breath away the night before.

"Now, we can't have that, can we?" His eyebrow arched at the glint in her beautiful eyes. Logan was more than happy to take care of all of Dallas' needs, but first, he'd need to—

His internal monologue was splintered by the sound of voices out to sea. They were faint but unmistakable—the sound of men shouting and cussing. Tensing, he eased her toward the equipment, his senses straining as he listened for more.

"Logan, I—"

"Shhh." He pressed his finger into her lips, effectively silencing her. "Are you expecting company?"

Dallas' brow furrowed. "No." Her voice had lowered to a murmur. "I don't hear anything."

"But I do." Like the rest of his unit, Logan's shark mutation heightened his senses, and even before he heard the telltale signs of people climbing onto the rig, he knew they weren't alone. "Let's go."

Abandoning the basket, he took her hand and encouraged her to the center of the rig. Logan's senses were poised and ready to decipher where the next clue would come from.

"Logan," she whispered, glancing back at him. "This is silly, I—" Her whisper was cut short as the illumination of a flashlight cut through the growing shadows. "Shit!" She gasped. "There's someone here."

"More than one person," he corrected, holding her close. "Stay close."

He didn't want to have to vocalize the thing he was sure they were both thinking—no one coming to an oil rig after dark had anything good in mind.

Tugging her down behind the huge equipment, he squeezed her hand. "We have to get off the rig."

"But, you have the only boat," she countered in a murmur. "And anyway, we don't know who it is. This is *my* rig, and I'm not abandoning it!"

"You'll do as you're told," he growled, exasperated that even in the face of potential danger, she was prepared to argue.

"Seems like the bitch is gone." The voice of a man he didn't recognize floated from the other side of the rig. "Just like the boss said she'd be."

Dallas' eyes were huge as she processed the words, and reaching for her face, he held her against him as the menacing stranger continued.

"Let's get on with it."

"For fuck's sake," grumbled another male voice. "Look how much paperwork there is here. What does he want with it all?"

"Didn't you listen?" sneered the first. "He wants it all destroyed."

Dallas gasped, her free hand rising to extinguish the sound.

"It's okay," Logan purred, wanting to soothe her. He may not have known Dallas for long, but he seemed highly attuned to her emotions, and as if he could hear her racing heart, he sensed her growing apprehension. "I have you. I'll keep us safe."

Though even as he made the claim, a surge of flames rose into the air on the other side of the rig, the noise and sudden illumination jarring his senses.

"Logan." Her hand clawed at his chest. "We can't let them destroy all the records. I'm not sure how all the dots connect, but they're linked to Green's murky operations."

Logan's focus flitted back to the angry flames. "I'm not sure there's much choice," he muttered. "They already have quite the bonfire going there."

In the haze of the embers, he could make out at least four men throwing paperwork into the fire.

"I'm personally not thrilled about Green destroying evidence, but my first priority is our safety." *Your* safety. He bit back on the words he really wanted to say. "That means getting off this rig."

Her brows knitted, and he could tell she wanted to counter the point.

"Baby." Grasping her face in his hands, he held her steady as he spoke slowly. "There is no democracy when it comes to your safety. I'm sorry you're upset about the records, and I understand, but we have no idea how many of these guys are on the rig. They could have found the boat, could have—"

"Hey, Jones."

Logan tensed as if he already knew what was coming next.

"There's a boat down here, some shitty little thing. Is someone else on the rig?"

"What?" cried the first male voice. "What fucking boat?"

"Come down and take a look for yourself."

"Fine, but the rest of you carry on. I want all this shit burned as soon as possible." There were mumbles of acquiescence from the others as the first guy, Jones, stalked off in the direction of the boat.

"Shit." Heart pounding, Logan assessed their options. "That settles it. We're getting off the rig, now."

"But how?" Dallas' breaths were coming hard and fast. "If they have the boat, then what do we do? It's too far to swim from here, and there are still some oil patches."

"Don't worry," he reassured. "Let's move, but quietly." Guiding her to the opposing edge of the rig, he spotted the emergency ladder down to the surface level. "There."

"But Logan!" She turned, exasperated. "We can't swim, I just told you. It's dangerous out there. This is a bad time of night to enter the water as all the predators come out to feed."

Logan suppressed the desire to laugh at her logical

concerns. You didn't need to worry about predators if you were swimming with one.

"Dallas, do you trust me?" In so many ways, it was a crazy thing to ask of a woman he'd only just met, a woman he had no rights over whatsoever, but Logan had no hesitation in asking.

"Yes." Her brow creased as though she couldn't believe her own answer. "Yes, I do."

"Then, trust me now." He pressed a chaste kiss to her forehead. "Climb down to the water level, and I'll be there in a minute."

Dallas blew out a breath, her gaze darting back to the unknown voices before she gripped the side of the ladder.

"Hold tight," he whispered, guiding her onto the first step as he pulled his phone from his pocket.

Guys,

He sent the missive on the group thread where any one of the five of the shark shifters could access it.

Dallas and I are on the rig
and we're in trouble.

He gulped at the words, calming his pulse as he checked on Dallas' progress.

Green has guys here burning evidence
and they've taken the boat.
We're gonna have to swim for it,
but I'm not sure how Dallas
will take the news.

Shit, this was not how he wanted to break the news of his abilities to her. He'd wanted it to be intimate and empowering, not fast and fearful.

Whoever gets this, I need you to
bring Top Secret to the rig and get us.

He could keep Dallas safe for a while, assuming she didn't die of fright first, but the water temperature wasn't ideal for late-night swimming.

As soon as you can.
Logan

"Logan!"

He glanced down at Dallas' concerned hiss.

"What now?"

Climbing lithely down to join her, he left his phone on a nearby metal ledge, inviting Dallas to do the same. Hopefully, they'd be able to salvage them both with the morning light, but one thing was for sure, Logan's escape plan would wreck their devices.

"I sent a message to *Top Secret*, but we can't wait for her to arrive. So, now we swim."

"But, Logan!"

"Baby." He sighed, wanting to simultaneously soothe and chastise her. "I can take care of you out there, and I've already asked the others to bring the yacht out to rescue us."

"You're a good swimmer?" She sounded understandably uncertain.

"The best." He flashed her a cocky smile. "But there's something else you need to know."

The sound of male voices grew louder above them, suggesting their foes were moving in their direction.

"Quickly!" she whispered. "Tell me. Whatever it is, just say it. I swear it won't matter. I won't judge you."

Taking her hand, he brushed his thumb lightly over her knuckles. How on earth was he ever going to make her understand?

"It's better if I just show you," he whispered, grazing his mouth over his lips. "I'm going to get into the water, and once I'm there, I need you to follow."

She nodded, clearly frantic with confusion. "Okay."

"Remember." He held her close, breathing in the tantalizing scent of her skin. "I won't hurt you. I'd never hurt you."

Puzzlement flashed in her eyes as he pulled away and stripped out of his shirt. A moment later, he slipped quietly into the water.

CHAPTER 17

Dallas

This was insane! There were men on board the rig destroying evidence and who knew what else, and Logan wanted to initiate some kind of intimate moment before they got in the water to be killed by sharks? Didn't he know the Sea of Cortez was full of all kinds of maneaters? An open fire on board an oil rig surrounded by the remaining slick caused by the spill was a recipe for disaster.

To think all she'd wanted when she spied Logan with a picnic basket was to get down and dirty on the main platform. It would have been epic and given her an amazing memory each day when she walked across the site. Her stomach grumbled—food would have been good right before he fucked her again. Yeah, that was the ticket: fuck—eat—fuck. How sick was it that Logan was proposing, no scratch that, commanding that they get into dark water full of oil and predators, men were onboard destroying evidence and who knew what else, and she was thinking about getting naked and nasty with her new hunky boyfriend?

Boyfriend? Was that what Logan was? Boy? There was nothing boyish about him. Well, that wasn't true. He did have the cutest boyish grin, as if he knew something nobody else did. Or maybe he shared it with his friends. The men in his unit, and their women, all seemed to be very close. It was nice to feel, for however long it lasted, as if she belonged with them as well.

She watched as Logan slid beneath the waves and waited for him to come back up. She was hoping he had some kind of jet propulsion unit to give them enough speed to get away from the rig. Dallas looked around to see if she could find SCUBA gear, a rebreather, or even a snorkel. No luck with the first two, but she did find a snorkel and mask. Maybe that would help. She put the mask on, securing it to her head before realizing that Logan would have no way to breathe. She removed the mask, wrapping the head strap around her wrist so it wouldn't get lost.

The men above her on the main platform were no longer trying to be stealthy. Their feet pounded against the steel grating that passed for flooring, and she could hear them swearing. Well duh! Light a fire on steel, and the steel was going to get hot. She touched the end of the platform above her. Shit! She pulled back her fingers. They hadn't had contact with the metal long enough to do lasting damage, but it hurt, nonetheless.

Dallas peered over the edge of the small loading platform. No sign of Logan. Oh God, had something happened to him? Then, as if to answer her question and her worst nightmare, a dorsal fin cut through the water. It was getting dark, but she could make out the distinctive crescent-shaped caudal fin, the larger of the two dorsal fins. Shit! A Shortfin Mako. Not what she wanted to see. They were swift, smart, and deadly.

Where was Logan? Had the Shortfin Mako attacked him? She looked around again. No bang stick, although they were fairly ineffective against the larger predatory sharks, but there was an underwater flare gun. Not sure what use it would be, but she shucked off her jeans and shirt, stowing them into one of the bins, secured the mask back on her head, and tucked the flare gun into her bra. She would remove the mask and share it and the snorkel with Logan when she found him. And she made herself think *when* not *if*.

She watched as the shark's fin cut through the water, showing that he was circling, which was unusual for a Shortfin Mako. They almost always attacked from below, taking chunks out of their prey's flank or belly. What was this shark doing cutting through the oil that still remained? She'd known sharks to swim deep below an oil spill, but most wouldn't swim through it, especially up near the surface where the crude was the thickest.

Dallas waited until the shark was at the upper end of his circuit, furthest away from the platform, then silently slipped into the water with her makeshift flotation device. She wanted to make the least amount of noise and disturbance in the water. The Styrofoam lid to one of the coolers wasn't ideal as a flotation device. It wasn't coated with anything to seal it, so it would eventually become soaked with water and oil and lose its buoyancy. But she was hoping, if she could avoid the Shortfin Mako, she could use it, so she could search for Logan and get them clear of the spill.

Where was he? Why had he left her? Why did the thought of him being gone make her heart ache?

She extended her arms, grasping the Styrofoam lid and putting her face in the water. She shivered with revulsion at the feel of the oil coating her skin, especially her face, but at least with the mask on, she could use the last of the waning light to peer below. She began to undulate her body like a dolphin, to move through the water. It was almost as effective as kicking but would create less movement in the water to hopefully avoid the shark's attention.

Dallas could see relatively little in the dark, oil-soaked water. She barely had time to detect movement and process the threat before the conically shaped nose of the Shortfin Mako bumped her in the belly. No, wait, that wasn't where he bumped her before moving off. She could barely see anything but was aware of movement in the water. Again, with little to no warning, the shark bumped her in her mons—almost as if he was aiming for that area. She wondered if she was bleeding out and if that was why she felt no pain from the bites.

Working hard to squelch the panic that threatened to envelop her, she continued to move through the water. Where was Logan? Why had she only now just met him to lose him? Could he somehow have been part of whatever was happening on the rig? Had he set her up? Another hard bump to her groin. What was this shark's obsession with her feminine parts?

As if to reinforce her conclusion about where it was aiming, it rubbed its entire body along her torso, wagging its head between her tits and swimming forward until it was beneath her body with its tail wedged between her legs, moving gently as if trying to arouse her. Okay, she had to be having the weirdest just before you die experience ever. She tried to move away from the shark, but it determinedly remained beneath her, its tail firmly in contact with her sex and its dorsal fin right in front of her.

The oil had helped the water to infiltrate the Styrofoam, and it was now becoming a liability. She could feel it starting to sink into the water and so released it. The shark batted it away with its head and then arched its back, so the dorsal fin was immediately in front of her. Tentatively, she grabbed hold of it, and the Shortfin Mako surged forward with a burst of blinding speed. She found it odd that the texture of his skin didn't cut or at least scrape her skin. She had always thought that shark skin would be rough. Dallas would have let go or tried to fall aside, but it seemed the shark had other ideas. Trapped between his dorsal fin resting in front of her head, whether she grasped it or not, and his tail up between her legs, if she didn't know better, she'd have sworn the damn thing was trying to stimulate her.

Dallas decided that as it seemed she had no choice but to do so, she grasped the shark's dorsal fin and clung to it for dear life, allowing her legs to further widen, so she was riding the shark versus being dragged by it. Sensing or feeling that she was more secure, the Mako took off, getting them clear of the oil slick and out into the clean water. It occurred to her that perhaps the shark didn't want to feed in hazardous water and wanted her flesh clear of the oily mess.

The shark rose closer to the surface, so she had no need for the mask or snorkel. Both were covered in black goo, so she tossed them aside. The shark continued to swim on what seemed to be a specific course. Where the hell was this thing taking her?

They had to be moving at close to fifty knots, which was absurd as Shortfin Makos were fast, but they weren't that fast, especially for a sustained amount of time. Yet, here she was riding along, cutting through the water at the same speed as a good jet ski. She had no idea where they were going or what the shark was doing. She'd never heard of a shark exhibiting this kind of behavior.

All she knew was the farther they got from the oil spill, the further she was from Logan. How was she going to get back? How was she going to find him? Could he even still be alive? She knew SEALs were excellent swimmers, but surely no one could survive in an oil slick for that long.

"Stop, please," she cried softly, and to her amazement, the shark did just that.

The shark circled around her, diving underneath her to ensure she remained on top of the water and to rub its body along hers. It was an odd sensation to be swimming in the dark night with a shark who seemed intent on saving her, and as if it could sense her distress, comforting her. It was almost as if the damn thing was trying to take care of her.

Dallas had never particularly wanted to be taken care of, but when Logan had asked that she trust him and declared that he would take care of her, it seemed to have been the thing she wanted most in life. Now, all she wanted was for Logan to be alive, hopefully sharing a life with her, but alive, nonetheless.

Letting her catch her breath, the shark moved back into position and waited for her to grasp his dorsal fin and wrap her legs around him. When she didn't, he used his tail to bump up against her pussy hard. While it was still arousing—which was definitely perverted—it also felt a bit like a disciplinary slap between her legs. When she didn't immediately move into position, the shark smacked her sex a second time—only harder.

Tentatively she grasped his dorsal fin and wrapped her legs around him. The instant she was secure, he put on a burst of speed on what she was sure was the same course as before. The shark was taking her somewhere—but where and to what end?

CHAPTER 18

Logan

All things considered, Dallas had taken his transmutation well. He wasn't sure if she truly understood that he was the shark, but she'd trusted the animal nonetheless, perhaps sensing he was her only route away from the danger of the rig. One thing was for certain, he'd certainly have to explain things to her properly once he was in human form again. But that could wait. For now, they were safe—he had kept her safe—and soon, they'd be back to the sanctuary of the yacht.

Flying through the water, Logan headed in the direction of *Top Secret*, but the vibrations in the water already told him that his message had been received—there was a large vessel cutting through the waves, and he was willing to bet it was the super yacht with his friends on board. He paused at the surface, judging their distance from the boat. It was approaching at speed, and he'd need to estimate its vicinity to make sure they were clear of its path.

"Oh God."

He stilled at the sound of her desperate sigh.

"Oh God, I left Logan. I can't believe I left him."

That confirmed it then. Dallas definitely hadn't put two and two together and figured out that he *was* the shark, but why would she? Dallas was a smart and determined woman, but she would never have believed men could shift into sharks. For the vast majority of people, that was just beyond what was conceivable. He didn't blame her for that, but he wanted her to know the truth, needed her to understand him. For the first time in his life, he craved that understanding, and he wanted Dallas to be the one who truly knew him.

He shook his head, wanting to console her and yet unable to do so as the shark. Much though he loved the feel of her splayed thighs against his back, he reluctantly accepted it was time to make the change. Searching the ocean, he spotted the vessel he'd sensed hurtling toward them. It would be alongside them before they knew it. The time to shift loomed—it was now or never.

Shaking her gently from his back, he watched her treading water before he dove into the deep. The water streamed over his gills as he surged back to the surface, breaching the waves with one dramatic splash. He morphed back to the man, knowing he didn't have long before the change overcame him again. Each species of shifter could last varying lengths of time before the urge took them, and fortunately for Logan, as well as being the fastest swimmer, he could also wait out the change the longest. Based on the speed of *Top Secret*, they wouldn't need that long.

"L-Logan?" Dallas' eyes were huge as she tried to process what she'd just witnessed. The enormous Mako who'd come to her rescue had just turned into her lover. "What the hell?"

"I know." He swam to her. "I know you're freaked out, but it's okay. I don't have time to explain now. We need to get on board." He motioned toward the incoming yacht. "Fast."

She nodded, clearly still shell-shocked by his sudden appearance, but understood what was required and trusted him to keep her safe. Reaching into her bra, she pulled out a flare gun, pointing it to the sky.

"Clever girl." Logan could have kissed her for her ingenuity. He didn't know where she'd got the flare gun from, but he loved her for having it. That was Dallas all over. She never disappointed.

She flashed him a salacious smile as she fired the flare. Swimming up behind her, he dragged her away from *Top Secret's* route, watching the final fireworks display in the sky overhead.

"Will they see it?" Dallas panted, obviously still perturbed about his altered state and yet equally anxious about the huge vessel speeding toward them.

"They'll see it." Logan had no doubt. His friends had seen his message, and their attention would be glued to the horizon. "Look, the boat's already slowing."

He didn't need to look to tell he was right; he could sense *Top Secret* decelerating. Sharks could detect motion for miles around, and his kind was more sensitive than most.

"Here!" Dallas waved her arms as she hollered, overwrought as the enormous yacht came to a halt a few dozen feet from them. Logan steadied her in the swell of water before motioning to the yacht's rear.

"Swim, baby." Logan encouraged her forward with a nudge. "Go around to the diving platform."

He waited as she swam around the vessel, sensing the first signs of the shift stirring in him. He had ignored the desire to transform for long enough, but while he would happily change back to the shark, he had to know Dallas was safe first.

"Logan?" She was close to the board as she called back.

"Go!" he ordered, breathing heavily as he fought to resist his natural impulses.

"Hey, Logan!" Nash called from the deck of *Top Secret*. "What happened?"

"Help Dallas."

Logan barely managed the words before the water blurred out around him, heat burning at his core. Vaguely aware of Nash's voice, he allowed the waves to swallow him up before the Mako Shark burst forth from within. Stretching out, he plowed through the water, darting toward the diving platform. Rising to the surface, he was pleased to see Dallas had already climbed on board.

"Come on, Logan." Zak gestured for Logan to come on board. "We're waiting for an explanation."

∽

Twenty minutes later, scrubbed clean and wrapped in a towel, he cuddled Dallas, who also had a towel wrapped around her, while the others quizzed them.

"They were burning evidence?" Trinity's alarm was obvious as she pushed a mug of hot tea with honey and lemon into Dallas' hands.

"That's right." Her jaw tightened. "Throwing it into the flames, and there wasn't a thing I could do…" Her voice trailed away.

"It's okay." Logan squeezed her softly.

"No, it's not," she insisted. "How will we ever be able to prove Green's link to all of this?"

"We'll find a way." Mason's tone was soothing as Dallas sipped at her drink.

"Thanks for coming for us." Dallas managed a

small smile. "I don't like to think about what would have happened if they'd spotted us on the rig."

"Logan wouldn't have let them hurt you." Flynn's reply was wry but knowing.

"No." Logan's arm tightened around Dallas. "I wouldn't have."

"I know." Dallas shifted in his arms. "But about that, can we talk?"

"I think that's our cue to depart." Zak chuckled as he took Trinity's hand and led her away. Logan watched as the rest of his friends and their ladies wandered from the salon, leaving him and Dallas alone.

"I'm sorry." Logan took her chin between his thumb and forefinger. "I never got a chance to explain."

Maneuvering from his digits, she kissed his knuckles. "Explain now, Sir."

Roused by her show of submission, he swooped, capturing her lips for a blissful, lingering caress. He needed that, the burgeoning intimacy, the undeniable connection they were building.

"I didn't want to have to tell you this way." Logan smoothed back her hair, inching closer until only their towels separated them. "But I had no choice. I needed the shark to save us."

"So, y-you're a shark?" Her voice trembled, her beautiful brows knitting as if she couldn't believe her own question.

"That's right." Stroking her nape, he went on. "I'm the Shortfin Mako."

"But, how?"

"That's a more complicated question." He chuckled. "And that doesn't mean I'm avoiding answering it either—I'm just saying—it's something we can discuss more as we get to know each other. It involves everyone on board here."

"All the others?" She glanced back in the direction of the exit though there was no one there. "You mean they can shift into sharks as well?"

Fleetingly, Logan contemplated the ethics of sharing this all with her but dismissed the idea as fast as it occurred to him. Dallas was already a part of their growing family. She knew his secret now, and he wasn't sorry that she did. The others would be fine with her knowing theirs too. Why else would they have welcomed her on board if that wasn't the case?

"Yes." He drew her closer and brushed his lips over her forehead. "All five of us SEALs."

"Wow." Her lips curled. "You're one hell of a special unit. Was that what Shiloh was talking about when she dropped me at the rig earlier?"

"Probably."

"Thank you for being so candid with me, Sir." She reached for his shoulder. "I've never met a man like you before."

"I'll always be honest with you, beautiful." Gratitude bloomed in his belly. He was so thankful to have found a woman who not only stimulated his mind but his cock as well. Even better, though, she was also excited by the same sexual proclivities that aroused him. It was the most peculiar thing, but he sensed they were meant to be together. A sacred feeling of knowing blossomed in his mind. This was right. It was meant to be. "I'll share everything with you."

It was crazy to make such a bold admission to a woman he'd only known for a day, but oddly, he didn't care. Every fiber of his being told him she was the one he'd been waiting for, and if Logan had learned anything from his genetic mutation, it was to trust his gut—to *always* trust it.

"This is a lot to take in." A wonderful blush bloomed on her cheeks. "But none of it helps us to uncover what's going on between Green and Effron."

"We'll figure it out," he assured her. "But we'll do it together."

"I like the sound of that." She leaned into him, and accepting her lead, Logan snaked his arms around her, holding her tighter. "And in the meantime?"

"In the meantime, let's take care of our needs." His lips twitched. "We'll eat, then go to bed."

"Are you instructing me to go to bed with you, Sir?" Her tone was playful.

"Oh yes," he purred. "You'll find my mutated genes mean I have one hell of an appetite for carnality."

Dallas licked her lips. "Maybe I need a spanking?"

He arched his eyebrow at her.

"I mean, I did stay late at the rig when I could have come back here earlier," she said with a shrug. "If I'd have done that, we wouldn't have had to swim for it."

"If you need a spanking, baby, then you don't need to justify yourself to me." Logan laughed. "You only ever have to ask."

CHAPTER 19

Dallas

Asking for something she needed had never come easily and asking anyone for a spanking was something she had never done. Unlike some submissives, she wasn't much of a people pleaser; she could say no. But asking for something was difficult for her. Why it seemed to come easy with Logan surprised her, but then if he was brave enough to share such a huge secret, how could she not admit her own vulnerability?

"You should know it's hard for me not only to acknowledge but admit that I need it even to myself. It's taken me a long time to get here."

He took her chin in between his fingers, forcing her to look at him. "You never, ever have to be afraid to tell me what you need. If it's within my power to take care of it for you, I will." He shook his head.

"What is it?" she asked, afraid he regretted ever meeting her, much less drawing her into his inner circle.

He brushed her lips with his. "Don't fret, I just keep having to remind myself that a week ago, I didn't even know you existed outside my fantasies…"

"Do I live up to your fantasies?" Her voice was unsure.

"No, baby. You exceed every single one. I would never have imagined the wonder that is you—and this isn't some line. You need to know that I… we… none of us ever brings a woman here just for casual sex. Okay, maybe when we first got the yacht, we had some parties that I'm sure were epic, if I could remember them. But once Mason met Shiloh, everything changed. It was as if seeing them together, seeing what was possible, made anything else seem like it wasn't worth doing."

Logan laughed. "And we knew something fundamental had changed when Zak brought Trinity on board the first time. He was trying to intimidate her, and he locked her in a cage…"

"He what?"

"Don't worry, and don't let Trin's diminutive stature fool you." He smiled. "That is one feisty, tough female. She is more than a match for her Tiger Shark mate. We were just figuring out about what went down the night the Admiral got assassinated…"

"I heard about that. I thought it was a botched hijacking…"

"That's what someone wants people to think, but none of us believe it. Flynn's girl, Devon, is a JAG lawyer who got sent to find out what happened, which leads me to tell you, at least until we figure this out, you'll be staying on the yacht, and you'll follow instructions, regardless of which member of the unit tells you."

"You do know I'm quite capable of taking care of myself," she replied. "I've been doing it for years."

"Yep, and you know I'm quite capable of delivering a discipline spanking you won't like in the least. Trust me, you do something you were told not to or put yourself in danger, and I'll leave a set of stripes across your backside that will last for days."

She sighed and sagged into him. "Why does that make me so goddamn horny?"

Logan stood up with her in his arms and headed back to their stateroom. "Because you were made for me."

Dallas waited for the fear and doubt to take over, assuming it would overwhelm her. It didn't. For some reason, this man, who had a strange mutation that allowed him to shift into a shark, made her feel safe, secure, and like she could do anything.

He shouldered his way into their room and closing the door behind them, he then set her on the bed. His towel was impressively tented, and she started to sink to her knees. She should probably see to his need before he saw to hers.

"Where do you think you're going?" he said, dropping his voice deeper in timbre and desire.

"I thought I would take care of that for you," she said, looking down between them at his stiffened cock.

"Who's in charge of this relationship, especially in sexual matters?"

"You are, Sir."

"Damn right I am. I have no trouble asking or demanding what I need or want from you. Right now, I need to see to your need to be spanked."

He kissed her long and hard before pulling her back, sitting on the edge of the mattress, and hauling her across his lap.

Grateful in a way she hoped she'd one day be able to express, she settled herself with a trembling sigh. "Thank you, Sir."

It had been an awful day. Someone was sabotaging the rig, Green and his cronies most likely, she still needed to contend with the spill, and someone was likely to be looking to get her fired or worse. She needed this—needed a reason to let go of all the stress and tension. She sensed he needed it, too.

When she thought of it, it seemed an odd way to connect, but every time Logan put his hands on her, she could feel that this was no casual interaction between them. This was momentous and right.

Logan reached up, unfastening her bra and letting

it fall to the ground as he slipped the towel from beneath her. Placing his hand in the small of her back, he brought the other down in a short, sharp arc that caused her to gasp from both the surprise and the sting. The cry quickly morphed into a long moan and then a sigh as she steadied herself by grasping his ankles.

He began to spank her in a slow, steady rhythm with just enough impact so she didn't feel he was playing, and that made her focus on herself and what it was doing for her. The only distraction was the throbbing promise of his cock beneath her. Over and over, he smacked her ass, the sound filling the room and surrounding her in a soft cocoon where everything was safe and nothing was impossible.

Dallas was aware of the pain, but more than that, she acknowledged the warmth and passion that flowed between them. She knew that however he chose to fuck her, her backside was going to hurt, but it was simply one more sensation to be embraced and enjoyed. Logan took his time, ensuring that not so much as an inch of her ass did not feel his strength and commitment.

In response, her body was languid and relaxed, her pussy ripe and wet. She moaned as she rubbed her cheek against his leg, drawing in her breath as his hand left her heated globes and found instead the warmth and readiness that lay between her legs.

He parted her labia, caressing her pussy and

drawing out her slick juices to coat her clit so he could provide her with added stimulation.

"Logan…"

He removed his hand and smacked her ass twice, once on each cheek. There was a definite difference in how he spanked her for stress relief or to increase her arousal and when he meant it for discipline.

"Sir," she corrected herself.

Logan's hand slipped back to the apex of her thighs, penetrating her with a single finger, gently stroking her and making her catch her breath. The spanking had primed her so well, she had to fight to keep from orgasming.

Again, the hand was removed, and he delivered another two stinging swats. "If I don't want you to climax, I'll tell you that, but there is nothing sweeter than the sound of your woman coming because you lead her there, and nothing feels better than having her pussy contracting in orgasm."

"I'm sorry, Sir."

"Don't do it again," he said.

Putting his hand back between her thighs and shoving two fingers up inside her, he thrust in and out so fast that she had no time to think, no time to protest, no time to do anything but be consumed by the powerful orgasm that washed over her, coating his hand with the depth of her pleasure. Her body clenched with her release and then relaxed.

Logan lifted her from his lap and settled her on

her back. She opened her arms, spreading her legs, a silent invitation to take what was his. She could admit now that she belonged to him in a profound and primal way she'd never felt with anyone else.

"Please, Sir…"

He cupped her heated globes in his hands and lifted her up as he impaled her with his cock. She had thought he might put her on her knees and take her from behind, but this was so much more intimate and did not diminish his power and control over her.

"Fuck, yes," he groaned.

His cock pressed deep inside her, and her pussy trembled all up and down his length. No one had ever made her feel like this—physically or otherwise. The feeling of being full of Logan was exquisite and carnal and something she never wanted to lose. He held her close, and her breasts were flattened against his hard chest. The tremble in her pussy became a whole-body shudder as he drove to her depths.

Dallas wrapped her legs around him, winding her arms around his neck. He kissed her passionately, possessively, as he lost control. He drew back and thrust into her. Finding a strong and steady rhythm, he began to fuck in and out, pounding into her and not allowing her to move with him. Over and over, he stroked her pussy as she climaxed again.

"That's my girl. Do you know how good you feel?"

She meant to answer him, but another shudder

seized her body, sending her over the edge into ecstasy. Logan hammered her pussy in a frenzy of need until finally, his entire body tightened as he ground himself against her, pumping her full of his cum before he fell on top of her, and she wrapped herself around him, offering him a safe, soft, warm place to rest.

When his cock had finally spurted the last drop of his release, he rolled from her, turning her away from him so he could pull her back against his body, spooning against her.

"Horny and tired," he mumbled before he began to softly snore—a gentle purr just next to her ear.

Dallas relaxed back into his body. There was a lot left unsaid between them, a lot unknown, but for now, they were safe, and whatever was coming would be easier to bear because it would be shared.

CHAPTER 20

*E*li Green
Green held the receiver to his ear, pleased to finally hear from his gun for hire, Mawnsey.

"It's done, Mr. Green." Mawnsey's rough tone echoed down the line. "It's all burned."

"You're sure?" Green turned as the brunette collapsed over the arm of his couch and moaned softly. She'd passed out exhausted after he'd finished with her ass, but if she didn't wake up soon, he'd be showing her the door. "All the evidence is gone?"

"Every last page."

"Any signs of USBs or disks that could have data saved on them?" Green knew he was being paranoid, but he didn't care. There was too much at stake to risk any loose ends. He never left anything to chance.

"I have everything with me," came the reply. "I'll bring it to you first thing."

"Good work, Mawnsey." He grinned, running his tongue over his teeth. "I'll see you in my office at nine."

Green ended the call, checking that the nameless brunette was still unconscious. Satisfied she wasn't privy to his conversations, he wandered to his enormous balcony, punching in the number for Admiral Wilson. The dial tone rang out for a few seconds, furling the tension in Green's belly before finally, a hoarse-sounding Wilson answered.

"Green? Do you know what time it is?"

"I'm not the speaking clock." He hadn't called to observe social niceties and sure as hell didn't appreciate Wilson's tone. The man owed him, and it was almost time to call in the favor. "I need your full attention."

"What's this about?" Wilson sounded more awake now, the anxiety in his voice pleasing.

"Our friends in the shark city."

Green's lips curled as he glanced out over the black ocean. Somewhere out there was a metropolis created and honed by the US Navy—the place they ran their genetic experiments. Green's organization had plowed a ton of money into the endeavors, which meant he knew all about the shark shifter trials, and he knew what the men and women in white coats intended to do next. Green had been one step ahead the whole way, and while it had been fun to watch the mad scientists play at his expense, he was getting tired of the game. When assholes like Logan Knight turned up at oil rigs and threw their weight around, it was time to remind them all who was boss.

"Wh-What about them?"

He definitely had Wilson's attention now. Admiral Wilson had been in charge of the entire Guardian Project for years, and while he liked to keep a low profile, Wilson remembered who signed the paychecks. He might technically work for the American government, but they both knew who was in charge.

"It's time we had another meeting." Green inhaled the sea air, strolling back to the bedroom to find his most recent piece of pussy sleeping like a baby.

"Why, is there a problem, Mr. Green?" Wilson's breath was ragged. "Something I should know about?"

"It's been a long time, is all." It had been too long. "I want to know what's going on down there. Where is all my money going?"

"I can have a progress report emailed to you first thing tomorrow." Wilson sounded panicked, and while the thought amused Green, it wouldn't be enough to placate him. Not this time.

"That's not good enough," Green informed him.

"I need to go there and see what's going on for myself."

"That's not so easy," Wilson started. "I'll need to get you clearance and ensure you—"

"Cut the bullshit, Admiral," Green interrupted. "We both know without my significant additional funding, this project wouldn't exist."

The silence on the other end of the line confirmed the point.

"I pay close attention to all of my investments and would like to meet with the scientists in charge of this one."

"Okay." Wilson exhaled. "I could have them brought to you in a couple of days? It would be a lot easier than bringing you down to the city."

"I'm not interested in easy, Admiral." Green's money ensured that case was always a given. "You and I both know I can make the demand. Your job is to make sure I get what I want seamlessly."

"I know my job, Mr. Green." The faintest edge of defiance burned in Wilson's response.

"Then, see to it." Green was fed up with having to babysit people who were old and ugly enough, to know fucking better.

"Who would you like to meet there?"

Now, that was more like it.

"All senior leadership personnel," Green answered. "Military and scientific. I want to know precisely what's planned, the timelines, and what return on my investment I can expect."

"You understand this is a US Navy site?" The glimmer of insolence in Wilson's tone was turning into something Green resented. "You do not have jurisdiction."

"Did I ever ask for jurisdiction?"

Green had endured enough of the Admiral's old boys network. It was time these old men discovered their daddy's trust fund and place in the country club wouldn't be enough to save them. There was new money in the world, cash that flowed from operations that would curl the hair of even the most corrupt and idle men—men like Wilson—and Green was one of those billionaires. He had no time and even less patience for their closed-rank mentality. They'd wanted his money, had turned on the charm to receive the initial investments, and he damn well expected reverence in return.

"Well, no, but—"

"Then that's not relevant, is it, Admiral?" Wandering into the bedroom, Green grabbed his bourbon, swirling it around the crystal as he stepped over the remnants of the brunette's attire. "I want an update—in person—or the funding will stop effective immediately." He paused, allowing that to sink in as he sipped at his drink.

"Now, there's no need for that, Mr. Green."

Wilson backtracked. "I'm sure I can arrange everything you require."

"Oh, I know you can," Green agreed, walking back to the balcony and looking out over the darkened gardens that led to the water. "Neither one of us wants to be publicly linked to dangerous and unethical experiments that are going on without the nation's knowledge, but at least Green Enterprises can blame funding mistakes on its accountants. I'm not sure you or the US Navy want to be tangled up in the fallout, though."

"There'll be no need for anyone to *know anything*." Wilson inhaled. "If you give me a few hours, I can confirm the details of the meeting *in* the shark city and make sure all relevant personnel attend."

"Excellent." Green couldn't help his grin. Finally, Wilson was starting to make sense. "Tuesday will work for me."

"Tuesday it is then."

Green could imagine the expression on the Admiral's face, but to Wilson's credit, his tone never let it show.

"I'm sure everyone will be excited to meet the donor who has so generously funded their work."

"Well, you know I'm not a man who seeks praise and validation, Admiral." If Green didn't know better, he was sure he sensed Wilson suppressing a snigger, but he chose to ignore the crude response. "It's enough for me to know I'm making a difference, and the Guardian Project *is* making a difference, isn't it?"

"Oh, absolutely," Wilson enthused. "It's groundbreaking research, the likes of which we've never known before."

"Then that's all I need to know tonight." Green drained the remainder of his glass. "Make the arrangements and send me the details."

"I will. Good night, Mr. Green."

"Good night."

Green cut the call, smirking as he placed the crystal on a nearby table. Now that he had that meeting in the works, it was time to dismiss his latest conquest.

"Hey." He nudged her shoulder as he passed the couch. She was attractive enough—he wouldn't have screwed her otherwise—but the mood had definitely passed, and now she was just taking up space. Green wanted to be alone. "Wake up."

"What?" She roused, her eyeliner smeared around wide, confused eyes as she lifted her face from the cushion.

"It's time to go." He gestured toward the door. "Get dressed."

"B-But..." She stammered, glancing around wildly.

"But nothing." He sighed, sensing his irritation rising. "Here."

Hooking her lace panties with the toe of his

expensive Italian shoes, he lifted the lingerie into the air and flicked them in her direction. They landed on her thigh.

"Put these on."

"Can't I stay a little longer?" she complained, struggling to slide the panties over her ankles. "I thought we had fun?"

"*Had* fun," Green reiterated, his patience wearing thin. "Emphasis on the past tense. I don't want to discuss it, darling. We've fucked, and now you can fuck off."

Green watched as her expression crumpled, wanting to roll his eyes. Women, like most men, were utterly fucking pathetic, and once their usefulness had worn out, he wanted nothing to do with them. He sighed as she collected her discarded clothes and hobbled toward the door. Couldn't she move any faster?

Turning to him, she sniffed as she grabbed her purse. "Bye then."

"Yeah." He didn't even glance in her direction, his attention already on the device in his hands. "Bye."

If her impending waterworks were supposed to tug at his heartstrings, then the needy little bitch would be disappointed.

Eli Green didn't give a shit, and he certainly didn't have a heart.

CHAPTER 21

Dallas

Her cell phone trilled in her ear. Damn, she'd forgotten to turn the ringer off. Wait, she'd left her cell phone aboard the rig last night when she and Logan had made their hasty escape. She grasped the phone where it lay on the bedside table. Logan's warmth was not at her back, and when she glanced around, he was nowhere to be seen. Ugh, it was Barney.

"Ms. Miles? There's been trouble on the rig. I know you worked late, but I think you need to come."

"What kind of trouble, Barney?"

"Looks like someone took a sledgehammer to a bunch of the stuff in the wheelhouse and then had a party on the main platform."

Even though she knew the answer, she asked, "what do you mean by that?"

"Looks like they had some kind of bonfire."

"Okay." She sighed. "I'll grab a shower and be there as quick as I can. Are the skimmers still working?"

"Yes, ma'am, but somehow the pump got turned back on. I sent a couple of the divers down to turn it off manually."

"Good thinking, Barney. See you soon."

She ended the call and looked at her text messages.

Went and got our phones.
Didn't think it would be good for
them to be found.
Had to go on patrol.
Will be back mid-morning.
Stay on Top Secret.
Miss you already.
Logan

Well, he was right about that. Their phones being found wouldn't have been good. She texted back.

Call from the rig.
I need to go.
I'll be safe.
Miss you too,
Dallas

She'd typed that last part in there automatically and then realized it was true. She'd missed waking up nestled in his arms, which was ridiculous given the short amount of time they'd known each other.

Taking a quick shower, she got dressed and headed up to the galley to get some coffee and see if she could catch a ride. When she entered the main salon, Trinity, Shiloh, Devon, and Nash were all having breakfast.

"Good! You're awake." Trinity smiled. "I made breakfast and had put some aside to reheat for you, but we just sat down, so it's still hot."

"Thanks. You didn't need to go to that kind of trouble," replied Dallas.

"No trouble. I like to cook, and I may as well make enough for everyone. The guys are usually knackered when they get back from patrol. They want to eat, fuck, shower and sleep, although not necessarily in that order."

Nash snorted. "I wonder if your men have any idea how you girls talk about them when they aren't here. Why did I get stuck staying here to play bodyguard?"

"Don't mind Nash," Shiloh snorted. "He seems to be in a peevish mood this morning."

"I am not peevish," he retorted.

Devon, who was sitting next to him, patted his arm. "Let's not put that to a vote, shall we? I don't think the results would do anything to soothe the deadly predator that lives inside you."

Dallas smiled. Nash was, by any standards, an imposing figure, but none of the other women were in the least bit intimidated by him.

Dallas sat down and began to eat the breakfast casserole Trinity had made. It was damn good. Dallas wasn't sure what Trinity did for a living, but she ought to be doing something with her cooking skills.

"This is delicious, Trinity. Can someone give me a lift out to the rig?"

"Logan wants you to stay here," Nash grumbled.

"I understand that," she implored. "But I have a job to do and already talked to the rig foreman this morning. That oil spill isn't going to get cleaned up without someone making that crew do their job. In case you missed it, that shit is damaging the ocean."

"I live part of my life in that ocean and have friends who do too. I am well aware of the damage your oil spill is doing to my ocean," Nash growled. "Until Logan tells me otherwise, you're staying here."

"No. I'm not. If none of you want to take me, I'll simply borrow one of the smaller boats and take myself. Actually, that's probably a better idea."

"No," Shiloh replied, "the best idea is to do as Logan asked. There may be more going on than we know about."

"And they tend to get pissy about any of us girls not doing as they wanted when they feel our safety is involved," added Devon.

"I get it, but it's my job, and it's not like Logan and I have even talked about a committed relationship…"

Trinity laughed. "Girl, if you haven't figured that out yet, you haven't been paying attention."

Dallas shook her head. "Doesn't matter. I'm going to the rig to see if I can't mitigate some of the damage."

Dallas finished her breakfast, grabbed a travel mug, filled it with coffee, and headed outside, walking toward the stern of the boat where a small powerboat and two zodiacs were tied up.

"Where do you think you're going?" snarled Nash.

"I think I'm going to the rig to do my job." Dallas' tone was even.

"Maybe one of us should come with," Trinity suggested, standing with Shiloh and Devon. "At least then you won't be all alone."

"Fuck it," said Nash. "You three get back inside, turn on the alarm system and stay put until the others get back. I'll take Dallas out to her rig and stay with her." He turned to Dallas. "But when Logan beats your ass for this, I'm going to tell him I get to watch."

Dallas smiled sweetly. "Not a problem. I've always had a bit of an exhibitionist streak." That wasn't strictly true. She had no trouble being naked around a bunch of people, but the idea of Nash watching as Logan roasted her backside and she got all aroused was not something she looked forward to.

"God save me," he grumbled, heading down to the power boat. "I thought I ordered you three to get back inside."

"Last time I checked, Commander, I was the only one in the Navy, which means you can't order anybody else, and you don't outrank me." Devon smiled as sweetly as she could muster.

"Women… give me a soft woman who knows her place."

"And where would that be exactly?" asked Shiloh.

"Most likely with her legs wrapped around his waist and his cock shoved up her cunt," Trinity said in a pleasant tone that belied her otherwise annoyed demeanor.

"In case you missed it, Dallas, Nash can be a misogynist pig when he tries, and we girls stick together," Shiloh responded. "I will say, if the rig is dangerous, it probably wouldn't be the worst idea to have him with you. While he might enjoy seeing Logan put you over his knee, he'd give his life to protect yours and would never lay a finger on you."

"You three, get inside, *please*. If we're going, let's go."

"Wait!" Trinity ran back to the galley while Nash helped Dallas aboard the powerboat. "Here you go, Nash. Part of that snarly countenance could be due to only one cup of coffee."

"Thanks," he mumbled as Trinity thrust the travel mug in his hand. "I don't know why Zak puts up with you."

"That's easy. Because I fuck even better than I cook," Trinity answered him with laughing eyes.

Nash worked hard to suppress his grin, then turned away, muttering something under his breath. Once Dallas was seated, he maneuvered the boat away from *Top Secret* and headed to the rig.

When they began to close on their destination, Nash turned to her, "I don't know if you were just deflecting, but even though he may not have said it, Logan is committed to you. We don't bring casual sex partners to *Top Secret*. We used to…"

"Logan mentioned you had some pretty epic parties in your wilder days."

He chuckled. "Yeah, plenty of debauchery, that's for sure. All I can say is when one of my unit decides he's found the one, they're all in."

"I kind of got that from some other things Logan has said, but it's just kind of weird, you know?" She shook her head. "It's like if I read it in a romance novel, I'd roll my eyes and think that it just doesn't happen like that."

Nash shrugged. "Sometimes it does. Sometimes it takes a lot longer, especially if a guy isn't out there looking for it, but sometimes I think the universe just hits a guy upside the head and says 'That's the one asshole. Go get her.' For what it's worth, all three of the others were pretty damn fast as well. We tend to be pretty laser-focused when we find the one. It's not every woman who can deal with the man in her life being a mutant."

Something about the way Nash said the last part

tugged at Dallas' heartstrings, and she suddenly understood why the other women weren't afraid of him and why they seemed to have genuine affection for him. As they pulled up to the rig, she put her hand on his shoulder and kissed his cheek.

"I feel the same way about him. I may not understand it, but I know what I feel. I would never do anything to hurt him." She squeezed Nash's arm. "And, you're not a mutant. None of you are."

Spying another powerboat, Nash cocked his head, "I wonder who else is here? Do you recognize the boat?"

Dallas shook her head. "No."

"Then I go first. You stay behind me. Got it?"

"Yes, sir," she answered, snapping him a quick salute.

"Don't get sassy with me. You're going to be in enough trouble with Logan as it is."

They had barely made it up to the main platform when they were confronted by Zander Effron, the company's CEO.

"You're late, Dallas." His tone was angry.

"I was here until late last night, so I slept in," she explained. "When Barney called, I headed right out."

"So, you admit you were on board alone after everyone had gone," the tone had turned accusatory.

She tried to move from behind Nash, who prevented her from doing so. "She was out here trying to clean up the mess your rig and your crew created.

She wasn't alone. She was with a member of the United States Navy. I'm Commander Nash Carlton, and you are?"

"I'm Zander Effron. I own this company. Your girlfriend…"

"Commander Carlton is not my boyfriend; another member of his unit is." Dallas inhaled. "And Nash, Mr. Effron does not own the company. His father does. Zander just runs it for daddy. I don't know why you're here…"

"Because I have information that says someone has sabotaged not only our efforts to clean up the spill but the rig itself." His eyebrow arched. "That information points at you, Dallas."

"Me? That's bullshit, and you know it. If you think you're going to hang this albatross around my neck, think again."

"I'll think whatever I like." Effron folded his arms. "I'm taking over the supervision of the cleanup and get this rig back online. I have looked at the records, including the times you've been written up for insubordination and anger management issues, and effective immediately, you're fired. You have until checkout time to remove your things from the hotel room or be liable for any costs thereafter. You're leaving."

Dallas tried to move again past Nash, who put his arm out to stop her. "Come on, Dallas, I'll take you back. We'll talk to Devon and figure this out. Don't worry, whatever these assholes are up to or are trying to cover up—we'll get to the bottom of it."

"Nash…"

"Now, Dallas."

The tone of his voice told her he wasn't taking no for an answer, that he had seen something he didn't like. He helped her down onto their powerboat, grabbing his cell and taking a picture of the other powerboat before speeding away from the rig.

"Take a deep breath, Dallas," Nash told her. "You're right, he's going to try to set you up. But we won't let that happen. Someone will go by your hotel and get your things. I want to take a picture of how we leave it, then we'll head back to *Top Secret*. Devon is one hell of a lawyer. She can't represent you officially, but she'll find the best person for the job and then oversee it to ensure it gets done right." Nash put his arm around her consolingly. "It'll be okay, Dallas. You're not alone anymore."

Dallas turned and watched as the rig shrank into the distance. She wanted to burst into tears but found Nash's presence comforting and realized she believed what he'd said. She would be all right. She was no longer alone.

CHAPTER 22

Logan

Hauling himself onto the yacht, Logan reached for a towel and strode on deck. Almost at once, he sensed something was wrong. He wasn't sure if he just had great intuition or if his mutation honed the skills, but his gut twisted in warning. *Something was wrong. Something was wrong with Dallas.* Heading for the salon, he noticed how tense and silent Devon, Trinity, and Shiloh seemed to be. Scanning the area, his worst fears were apparently realized—both Nash and Dallas were missing.

"Where's Dallas?"

All three women turned at his question, Shiloh rising to greet him. "Logan, you're back early."

His brow furrowed. That was a strange opening. He was the fastest swimmer and was usually the first back after patrol. Ignoring her comment, he wandered toward her. "Shiloh, where is she?"

"Don't freak out." Devon sighed. "She went back to the rig."

"She went back to the what?" Logan couldn't believe what he was hearing. Hadn't he specifically told her to stay on *Top Secret*? What on earth had Dallas been thinking?

"Yeah, Nash figured you'd react that way." Trinity smiled. "That's why *he* decided to take her."

"Nash has gone with her?"

He blew out a breath, his mind racing. A part of him was furious that his friend would be so reckless as to allow Dallas to leave, but then he knew what Dallas could be like. Headstrong and determined, she might not have given Nash much choice, and Logan knew his friend would never do anything to harm his woman. Secretly, he was relieved Nash was there to support her. Last night had proven that the rig was a perilously unsafe place for Dallas to be alone, and whatever she was doing, she'd be better off with Nash on her side.

"Yes," Shiloh confirmed.

"Yes, what?"

Shiloh leapt at Mason's voice, smiling as her lover entered the salon. "I was just telling Logan here that Nash has taken Dallas back to the rig."

"Really?" Mason's eyebrow arched, his arms

snaking around Shiloh as he met Logan's gaze. "And how's Logan taking that news?"

"He's not thrilled." Logan's voice was clipped as he wandered to the window and stared out at the endless sea. Even knowing Nash was with Dallas wasn't enough to assuage all his fears. She shouldn't have gone. She should have listened to him. "I think it's time I let Dallas know what happens to little girls who disobey."

"Oh, she knows." Trinity sniggered. "Nash warned her you'd yank her straight over your lap and tan her hide. He said you'd probably let him watch!"

"Good idea." Logan's jaw clenched as he fought to contain his irritation.

"What's happening here?" Zak strolled on board, heading straight for Trinity. Taking her face gently in his palms, he kissed her possessively, not caring that the others were all there to watch.

"Dallas has gone back to the rig," Devon explained from her seat. "And Logan isn't happy about it."

"I bet." Turning to Logan, Zak went on. "Want to head out and check on her?"

Logan sighed. "Badly, but Nash is with her."

"Then she'll be okay," answered Flynn, catching up on proceedings as he greeted Devon. "You know Nash will protect her."

"I know," Logan replied. "But…"

"Hang on!" It was Shiloh who spotted them, pointing out at the deep blue. "Isn't that their boat?"

All eyes fixed on the spot on the horizon, and Logan's heart pounded as he watched it grow bigger. It sure looked like the boat from *Top Secret*, and rushing out onto the deck, relief flooded Logan's system as he was finally able to make out Nash and Dallas. He hurried to welcome them, watching as Nash maneuvered the small boat.

"Logan." Nash rose, helping Dallas to her feet. "Before you say anything, I didn't have any choice. She was hellbent on going."

"I can imagine." Logan folded his arms across his chest, relishing the pools of heat blooming on his little girl's face. "Anything you'd like to say, Dallas?"

Dallas moved toward him, taking his hand. "Logan." She pulled in a shaky breath. "I…" Her voice trailed away as tears filled her eyes. Sweeping her from the boat, he pulled her flush against his chest, wrapping his arms around her as she started to sob.

"What the hell happened?" Logan demanded, his focus flitting from Dallas to Nash.

"Some asshole called Effron was on the rig." Nash stepped up beside them. "He tried to blame Dallas for what happened last night and proceeded to fire her."

"He did what?" Devon's voice cut through the strained atmosphere.

By now, everyone had come out to greet Dallas

and Nash, but it was Devon who stepped forward, her brow creasing as she continued.

"He can't just summarily dismiss you, Dallas."

"Apparently, he didn't get the memo." Nash patted Dallas' shoulder sympathetically as he walked past. "He's an arrogant sonofabitch."

"He doesn't even own the company." Dallas sniffed, drawing away from Logan enough to speak. "He has no freaking right!"

"Don't worry," Devon soothed. "Let me look into it. I'll nail that jerk to the wall for this."

"Thanks, Devon." Dallas managed a small smile. "Nash said you'd be able to help, and thank you as well, Nash."

"You're welcome." Nash nodded. "Although the deal still stands, I wanna be there when Logan puts you in your place for that little jaunt."

"About that…" Logan's voice lowered. Capturing Dallas' chin between his finger and thumb, he forced her attention to his face. "We're going to talk about your decision to leave the yacht when I told you to stay on board."

"I had to go." She wiped away her tears with the heel of her hand. "It's my job, or…" Her brow furrowed. "It *was* my job."

"It wasn't safe, baby." Logan stroked the side of her damp cheek. "Men like Effron are dangerous. He's probably in bed with that nefarious bastard, Green."

"Urgh." Zak screwed his face into a ball. "That's not a pretty image."

"But Logan's probably right," Mason continued. "I see Green's grubby paw prints all over this."

"All over what?" Flynn asked.

"The oil spill, the incident last night at the rig…" Mason shook his head. "All of it seems suspicious."

"I agree," Dallas mumbled into Logan's chest.

"Then all the more reason to stay clear of this Effron." Logan's tone told her that wasn't a suggestion.

"I know his father," Dallas replied. "I respect him. Maybe if I call him, I could—"

"No, baby." Logan's hand slid into her hair and tightened. "Let Devon do her job and investigate all of this first."

"Logan's right." Devon's tone was almost apologetic, as if she was letting down their new sisterhood by agreeing with one of the men. "Let's find out where you stand before we speak to Effron senior."

"Okay." Dallas looked lost as she ceded, her hand rising to her temple. "I have a headache."

"Let's get you something for it." Drawing her closer, Logan kissed her forehead. "And for the record, that's the only reason you're not sprawled over my lap right now."

A deeper blush pooled on Dallas' flustered cheeks. "But sir, I thought I was doing the right thing."

"Bullshit." Logan shook his head. "You knew

going back would land you in trouble—you knew it would upset me—but you went, regardless."

"Not to hurt you," she insisted.

"Maybe not." He met her watery gaze. "But there are rules on board this yacht, baby, and there are rules when you're part of this family, and one of them is that you Do. As. You're. Told." Logan accentuated the final words. "Especially when your health and safety are in question."

"Is that what I am?" Dallas glanced around, her expression almost awestruck. "A part of this family?"

"Of course!" Logan laughed gently, brushing his lips over her mouth. "Why else would everyone be here giving a shit? Why else would Nash have accompanied you and Devon offered to help?"

He glanced around to find them all there, smiling at his explanation.

"Logan's right." Zak took Trinity in his arms. "When you're with one of us, you *get* all of us."

"Oh." Dallas sniffed. "I've never been part of something like this before."

"She knows, right?" Nash's brow rose as he motioned toward Dallas. "She knows we're all shifters?"

"Yeah, she knows." Logan's fingers tightened, eliciting a tiny gasp from Dallas as he held her close. "Not all the details, but she knows about the mutation."

"You're definitely one of us," Mason added. "There's no getting away now."

"I don't want to get away." Her green eyes met Logan's, and slowly, his digits relaxed. "I'm so thankful to have met you all."

"Let's get you that headache remedy." Logan's arm snaked to her waist, guiding her toward the salon. "We'll talk about your punishment later."

"Make sure I get an invite." Nash laughed. "Unlike the rest of you, that's the most fun I'll get for a while."

"Don't worry." Logan glanced back to lock gazes with Nash. "You'll have a front-row seat, Nash."

"Welcome to the family, Dallas." Nash grinned as she turned to acknowledge him. "I can't wait to see your ass get blistered."

CHAPTER 23

Dallas

It felt good to be back in Logan's arms, back aboard *Top Secret*, and to have a family. She'd been on her own for so long that it felt good to be part of something—a group that cared for one another in a way that was more than just sex.

"Dallas, wait up!" called Devon as she ran toward her with Flynn following close behind.

"Devon, leave them be."

She skidded to a stop alongside Logan and Dallas before turning back to Flynn. "He can beat her ass later. This is important. Dev, did you file any reports about what you've been doing since you got here?"

"Yes," Devon replied. "I have to file daily reports, and I sent a memo to both HR and senior management about what I found the day I arrived."

"Good." Devon nodded. "Let's go see if we can

still get you on the company's computer system. If we can, I need you to file a report about what happened yesterday and this morning and your concerns about the state of the spill and nothing being done about it. Then we're going to print them all so that they are time-stamped."

"What good will that do? It's obvious they mean to blame me."

"Yes, but we're going to cut them off at the pass, so to speak." Devon smiled. "Once we have what we need, I'm going to call a few friends in the media, and you're going to go on camera and let the world know. We'll have evidence that might not work in court, but trust me, it will exonerate you in the minds of the public."

Flynn laughed. "You get 'em, baby." The pride in how quickly Devon's mind worked was apparent.

"Can we do that?" asked Dallas.

"We can if we hurry. They may not have cut you off from the computer. Let's go." She called back over her shoulder, "Babe, don't we have a secure connection here that they can't trace back?"

"Yep," Flynn sighed. "All I want to do is shower and fuck, but I have to go play computer nerd."

Logan laughed, and the two of them jogged to catch up with their girls.

Dallas had not been locked out of the system. She logged into it and wrote a report about being on board the night before, trying to make sense of the maintenance records and how the spill had happened in the first place. She detailed Logan coming to join her and their hearing people coming aboard.

"Make sure you convey they had no right to be there, and you and Logan felt your lives were in jeopardy and that you had to move off into shark-infested waters in order to ensure your own safety. Give the report and especially the memo a little drama," prompted Devon.

"You don't know there were sharks," Flynn queried.

"Of course, there were. Logan was with her. Well, maybe she should skip the part where she knows said shark intimately."

"Devon, behave yourself."

Devon looked at him with a wicked grin. "Not for much longer, *Commander*," she said, stressing the last word. "You're not the only one who wants to fuck."

Flynn rolled his eyes but said nothing.

Devon looked to Logan, who answered her unasked question. "Flynn was just recently made Commander, which gave him a rank equal to Devon's, which smoothed out the bump of her outranking him, which they will no longer court martial you for, but is frowned upon and could have earned Devon a written reprimand on her permanent record."

"Man, you type fast," Devon exclaimed.

"Yeah. I took a typing class in college. I thought it

would be an easy A; it wasn't, but it's helped me to get things done over the years."

"I also want you to fire off a memo to the Chairman of the Board and cc the rest of the Board about what happened this morning and your concern, regardless of what happens to you, about the oil spill. I want you on record as having expressed your concern for the environment."

Dallas laughed, starting not only to believe she might have a way out of this nightmare but having some fun along the way. "I may type fast, but your mind works at the speed of light."

"That's because she gives the hamsters amphetamines," quipped Flynn. Devon glanced over her shoulder at him as she elbowed him in the rib cage. "Sorry, semi-private joke. We'll fill you in later."

Dallas finished and filed her online report on the company's system and printed out all the documentation, showing the time and date stamps she had on the spill, including her notes and research, and then wrote a report for what had happened last night. She was just starting her memo to the Board when she was locked out of the system.

Chewing her bottom lip, Dallas glanced at Devon. "I was expecting that," said Devon. "I'm glad we got your official reports and notes entered and were able to get proof of when that was done. It'll be harder for them to blame you when we have evidence that contradicts that. Go ahead and do the memo to the board. I want you to be clear about what happened last night and this morning and how you are more worried for the environment than your future with the company."

"I'm also going to express that I question Junior's ability to lead the company as well as his ethics in getting involved with one of the largest shareholders in something that seems, at least from the outside, to be somewhat shady," said Dallas.

"Nothing like having your girl train their crosshairs on us," quipped Flynn.

Within the hour, they had all the documentation needed. Dallas had sent her separate memo to the Chairman of the Board, the Board itself, and her HR file. It too had been saved to the thumb drive, which was secured in a hidden safe, aboard *Top Secret* after two copies had been made—one going to the safe on board Shiloh and Mason's boat and one to be sent to an offshore storage facility that specialized in safe-guarding sensitive information. All the documents had been printed, showing their time and date stamps.

Trinity stuck her head into the room, "Can you take a break? I've got breakfast ready."

"Great timing," Devon grinned. "You go on. I need to make a couple of calls…"

"You need breakfast," said Flynn, "then I need to fuck…"

Devon turned to him, rubbing her body against his. "I tell you what, why don't you go get some food to take to our room and I'll meet you there in nothing flat. That way, I can take care of both of our dual appetites."

"She's leading you around by the dick again." Logan laughed at Flynn.

"That's all right. It's where I wanted to go, anyway, and it gives her a feeling of still being in command, which she isn't."

Logan chuckled, leading Dallas out of the computer station. "That was Devon, showing you the art of negotiation, but don't try that topping from the bottom shit with me. All you'll get is a very sore bottom."

"I didn't mean to upset you," Dallas murmured.

He nodded. "I know, baby."

"It's just the spill…"

Logan stopped, turning her so that her back was flat against the wall and holding her there. "I know, but the fact is I told you to stay put, and you disobeyed me, thereby putting Nash in the position of having to leave the other girls here so he could keep you safe. We have a hell of an alarm system, and personally, I wouldn't want to go up against Trinity, Devon, and Shiloh. But you placed Nash in an untenable position of having to try to keep them safe on board while he chased after you."

"I'm not being resistant to discipline; I just don't think it needs to be shared."

Logan laughed. "*Shared* is my strapping you down

to the spanking horse and letting the Bull Shark smack your ass until he feels you've atoned for what you did to him. This is more like witnessed. You ask Trinity about what happens when little girls misbehave in public, especially when it's blatant disobedience. The first time I met Trin, she was face down over Zak's knee getting her backside blistered."

"Why does he want to watch?" Dallas huffed.

"First off, most guys have a voyeur streak, or at least all of us do. Second, you not only disobeyed me, but you also wronged Nash. There are some times when I'm sorry just isn't enough. This is one of those times."

"But just Nash, right?" Her brows knitted.

"That's going to depend. I won't ask any of the others to watch, but I will let them know they are welcome to do so. After all, Nash having to take you to the rig meant he wasn't on board with them."

"Why is that so important?" Dallas knew she was whining, but bad as it was to think of Nash getting to see her get spanked, it would be a lot worse if they all did.

Logan took a deep breath. "Things are moving fast, and we have so many irons in the fire. You heard about the admiral who got killed, right?" She nodded. "We were on board for that party. It wasn't just a random terrorist attack. The people behind it, and we don't know who they are, have made a couple of attempts on our women, so we've closed ranks. Nash had to go with you, which left them vulnerable, not overly so, I'll admit, but still, I told you to stay put for your own and their safety. The guys are entitled to see you punished for that behavior and in a way that makes them believe you won't put their women in danger again."

Much as she hated to admit it, he had a point.

"Okay. I guess I can see that's only fair. But I did lose my job this morning."

Logan laughed, which made her feel inordinately better. "That's not much of a mitigating circumstance since you weren't going to be working for them much longer. They're a sleazy company, and you deserve better."

"I have bills to pay…"

"And a man who makes more than enough money to pay them."

That stopped her cold in her tracks. "Really?"

"Really. I told you I'd take care of you. I know you well enough to know that you're going to want to work, which is fine, but only for a company I approve of doing something that won't get you killed."

"But you could be killed doing what you do," she complained.

"Yes, but mine isn't a job, it's a duty and part and parcel of what I signed on for."

He turned her toward the salon and smacked her ass to move her forward.

"I don't suppose that will suffice for discipline?" she asked hopefully.

"Not a chance. When I get done with you, you're going to have a bright red ass and think twice before putting yourself and others in danger."

CHAPTER 24

Dallas Logan waited until after lunch. Dallas was calmer and more content now that Devon was on the case of Effron's murky endeavors, but more than that, she was well-fed, watered, and her headache had abated. He caught her wrist when she started to help Zak, Trinity, and the others clear the table after the meal. Pulling her back to her seat, he leaned close.

"Where do you think you're going?"

Dallas turned to him with wide green eyes. "Tidying after lunch." Then, as if she tuned into his mental process and knew what he was thinking, she added, "Sir."

"Not this time." Logan tugged her closer. "The others will have to do without our help."

"Are we finally gonna get a show?" Zak's tone was wry as he collected unused cutlery.

Logan's gaze flitted to Dallas before he replied. "If you want one, but the front seat is already promised to Nash."

Returning from the basin, Nash's grin grew. "About time." He clapped his hands together. "I was starting to think you'd gone soft, Logan."

"No way." Logan's attention never diverted from Dallas' face. "I just had to give my angel a while to settle first."

"Oh, boy." Flynn chuckled. "It sounds as though you're not going to enjoy this much, Dallas."

"Do they all have to watch?" Dallas squirmed in her seat, heat flaming in her face.

"We talked about this." Logan's voice was even, his grip on her wrist relaxing. "They have a right."

"I know, but…" Dallas sighed, evidently struggling with the right words. "This is so mortifying."

"For what it's worth, my advice is just to ignore them all." Trinity offered a sympathetic smile. "Focus on Logan."

"Oh God." Dallas closed her eyes. "You're really going to do this." Her tone suggested it was more of a statement than a question.

"I'm really going to do this." Logan drew her closer, skimming his mouth over her lips until her eyes flickered open. "We both know you deserve it."

Silence bloomed between them, the others stilling to acknowledge the burgeoning intimacy between the new couple.

"Come on." Logan's murmur broke the quiet, and with one sharp yank, he hauled Dallas from her chair and over his lap.

Lifting the long skirt she'd borrowed from Shiloh, he bunched the fabric around her middle, running his palm over her goosing flesh.

"The show is finally getting started!" Pulling up the chair Dallas had vacated, Nash settled opposite them. "Let's see if you can't teach this little lady the merit of obedience."

"Indeed." Logan lifted his palm, smacking it down on her prone ass. At his request, she wasn't wearing any underwear, and the strike resounded around the large room. "That was one, Dallas. You can count them for us."

"Oh God." She sucked in air, her hands balling into fists at his command.

"What was that?" Logan swatted her harder, enjoying her frantic wince.

"Two, Sir," she replied, writhing over his knees.

If Logan didn't know better, he'd have sworn she was thrashing about just to arouse him further. Her struggles were definitely doing something for him, whether she intended the effect or not.

"Better."

He peppered her backside with short, insistent smacks, ensuring every inch of her skin was tanned. Dallas numbered the strikes as best she could, unable to keep still as the spanking was delivered. It was obvious to Logan that Nash's enthusiastic audience was making the whole ordeal harder for her to bear, and all the while, those who weren't relishing the show went about their business, clearing the table and loading the dishwasher.

Good. He smiled, bringing his palm down against her heating skin. His palm covered her ass in unyielding spanks, ignoring her frantic whimpers. *The more embarrassed Dallas is, the longer the lesson will linger. She'll think twice before she runs off and puts herself in harm's way again.* He intended to soothe and love her after the spanking was over, but he didn't want there to be any doubt. Dallas was his woman now, and that meant she would cede to his will when her wellbeing was involved. It also meant if her actions endangered the wellbeing of other people in the group, she would pay the price. Logan would worship and adore her but wouldn't hesitate to bring her back into line.

"Thirty, sir," Dallas gasped, one of her hands rising to cover her coloring backside. "Please, stop!"

"No." Grabbing her wrist, he shifted it against her lower back, pinning her in place. "We're nowhere near done, are we, Nash?" Logan glanced up to meet Nash's smirking expression.

"Not even close." Nash leaned forward, eyeing Dallas' pink skin.

"You gotta learn the lesson, baby." Logan spanked her again, focusing a flurry of swats on one cheek until she cried out.

"Logan!"

"Wrong answer," Logan growled, shifting his palm to the sensitive underside of her behind.

"Sir, I'm sorry, but please, it really hurts!"

"It's supposed to hurt." Nash leaned back in his seat, his lips curling. "That's how you remember and learn from the experience."

"You heard the man." Logan struck her other cheek, relishing the look of the impact reverberating around her body as she choked out the appropriate number.

He couldn't lie. Logan was reveling, not only in the honor of spanking Dallas' fine ass but also in the performance he was putting on for his friend. She had been a complete brat to Nash, and he deserved to witness her flaming ass and to know Logan had reiterated the message with the punishment. Looking up, he noticed Zak and Mason had come over to take in the sight of the upturned Dallas. Only Flynn and the other ladies had busied themselves elsewhere.

Rubbing her tender flesh, Logan met the men's eyes in turn. "How many do we think she warrants?"

"At least fifty for endangering herself." Mason's reply was unequivocal.

"I agree." Zak folded his arms across his chest. "Plus more for leaving Shiloh, Devon, and Trin alone while Nash went to babysit."

"Oh yes." Logan squeezed her toned orb, his lips curling at her breathy mewls. If he didn't know better, he could have sworn his little girl was actually enjoying her penance. Sure, he wasn't going easy on her, and he accepted that she'd never admit to relishing a single second of the experience, but he was willing to wager that when he slipped a finger between her legs, he'd find a warm and welcoming reception. "Definitely more for that. How many swats was that, baby?"

He released the pressure on her wrist, permitting her arm to fall down to the floor as she answered.

"F-Fifty, Sir."

"Another twenty-five then, gentlemen?" Logan addressed the assembled men, smiling at their considered verdicts.

"Seems fair," Mason nodded.

"It's your show." Nash gestured toward her reddening ass. "I'm just here to enjoy it."

"Oh God." Dallas heaved in a shaky breath.

"I didn't ask for your opinion, young lady." He spanked her exposed ass hard. "And that strike doesn't count toward your tally."

"I'd have gone higher myself." Zak's eyebrow arched. "But she's coloring fast, and Nash is right; this is your show."

"Right." Logan grazed his heated palm over her upturned backside. Dallas was so fucking gorgeous, but Zak was correct; her skin was redder than he'd imagined it might be at this juncture. "We need to build your tolerance for spanking, baby."

"Not like this," she pleaded. "Please, Sir."

Logan laughed. "If you don't like being the object of everyone's fascination, you'll have to make sure you don't endanger the others again."

"I thought you said you had an exhibitionist streak, Dallas?" Nash's lips twitched, his focus falling to her face, most of which was hidden by a curtain of her strawberry blonde mane. "That you didn't mind people watching?"

"Not like this." She sounded anguished. "Never like this."

"Come on." Logan patted her ass gently. "It'll be over soon enough."

"Too soon for my liking," Nash chuckled.

"We've got to get you together with that doctor you're interested in, Nash," Mason smirked. "You're starting to sound desperate."

"Fuck you!" Nash spun in his seat, spitting the curse at Mason. "I don't need any help where women are concerned."

Logan raised his palm, smacking Dallas hard and drawing all of their concentration back to the matter in hand. "Excuse me, gents, but we're not done here."

All three sets of eyes returned to him.

"Be our guest." Nash motioned for Logan to continue.

"Thank you, how many, Dallas?"

"Fifty-one, sir," she mumbled just loud enough to spare her additional swats.

"Then I have twenty-four left to deliver."

Logan ran his hand down the cleft of her ass, noticing the way her breathing accelerated. Dipping one digit past her labia, his cock stiffened inside his pants. Her pussy was glistening with need; evidence that, just as he suspected, she was enjoying the punishment—whatever she had to say on the matter. He couldn't wait to take her down below and screw her after this, to fill her up and confirm what they both already knew. She was his, and they belonged together.

"Twenty-four tough strikes and I intend to enjoy each one."

CHAPTER 25

Dallas

Dallas hadn't signed up for this. She knew her face had to be as red as her ass. If she was being honest with herself, the thought of Logan playing with her had been arousing, maybe even a light spanking, but turning her backside all kinds of red? It hurt. It hurt a lot. But the worst part was it also had her so turned on she didn't know what to do with herself.

Her entire body shivered—not from cold but from pure arousal—as he ran his finger down the cleft between her burning cheeks, stroking her puckered entrance before parting the petals of her sex and finding the shameful proof of her need for this man, for his discipline and for his touch.

Having the others watch and casually discuss things with Logan was mortifying in the extreme.

How would she ever look these men in the face again? Logan continued to smack her ass as she counted out the last twenty-four painful strikes.

At twenty, he said, "Spread your legs, Dallas."

His voice was soft, but the resolute tone behind his words let her know his words were not a request but a command. She flushed beet red with humiliation. She wasn't cut out for this. She couldn't be; she didn't want to be. But was that true? Hadn't Logan been everything she'd always wanted? Hadn't he fulfilled every fantasy? The answer was yes to both questions. She knew it had only been a very short while, but the growing intimacy as well as the depth of feeling only confirmed that much as she hated the idea that she did, she needed him in a way she had never needed anyone before.

"Now, Dallas," he commanded.

She sighed deeply and let loose the last remnants of her stubborn pride, giving over and opening for him.

"That's my good girl," he crooned, and she knew he wasn't talking about her obeying the actual command but what it signified.

Her body sagged against his leg. Logan drew his fingers through her swollen and wet labia, trailing them through the wealth of moisture he found there and taking it to her clit. With infinite deliberateness, he circled and rubbed her little nub, chuckling with a possessive male authority she found delicious.

He lifted his hand and brought it back down on her sex, just as hard as the strikes to her backside. It made a noisy, wet splat that stung like blue blazes. She knew the last five he felt she was owed would be delivered to her pussy and that she would be sore, but she didn't care. Didn't care that she could hear the sharp intake of breath coming from Nash. All she could feel was the way the punishing caress sent bolts of electrifying arousal straight to her pussy.

"Seventy-five," she called out. "Sir, please."

"You want me to take care of you, angel?"

"Please, sir."

"Right here?"

"Yes, please."

"Well, gentlemen." Logan's voice was gleeful. "I know I'm satisfied or will be shortly, but Dallas didn't just endanger herself, did you, baby?"

"No, Sir."

"Then you apologize to them."

Logan played with her pussy while he talked to her, and the increasing arousal was leaving her on the cusp of an orgasm. She was certain he was aware of that fact and his show of mastery over her, and her body was part of the message—not just to her but to the men in his unit.

Taking a halting breath, she steeled herself, "I'm sorry that my rash actions put my friends in danger. I'm sorry that Nash had to risk himself and the others to keep me safe."

"Good enough?" he asked his friends.

"Almost," Nash said harshly.

She glanced up from beneath the curtain of her hair to stare at the bulge that pressed against the front of Nash's fly. It served the sonofabitch right to be as aroused as she was. The difference was Logan would see to her need while Nash would have to see to his own.

"Finish her," whispered the brute, who had shown her a tender side earlier.

"I'd planned to," said Logan as his cock throbbed beneath her.

Oh, God, he wasn't going to… two of Logan's fingers penetrated her core, and she bit back a scream of need.

He didn't say a thing, just thrust his fingers in and out of her wet heat as her climax began to overtake her. Her inner walls trembled as she tried to rationalize the intensity of the pleasure. There were people —men—watching her, and even though Mason, Zak, and Flynn had acted as observers, they were now viewing the proceedings with intense attention.

Dallas' breath sped up, and she couldn't hold back the whimpers that made their way past her lips as Logan stroked her, calling forth her response to him as he did so. Her orgasm approached faster than she could comprehend. It made no sense. She should have been so mortified, but she wasn't. She was on fire—a wildfire burning out of control that only he could truly quench. That wouldn't be completed here, but he would force her capitulation to his authority.

Her body stiffened as the whimpers became moans, and her breathing became erratic and thready. The sheer terror and exhilaration she felt under his command were breathtaking. It was embarrassing that he could undo her to this extent, especially in front of an audience. Maybe she was far more of an exhibitionist than she thought. Suddenly the idea of climaxing in front of these men was not only wildly arousing but was also their due. She finally grasped the idea that for them to feel as though they could trust her with their women, they had to know that she submitted to Logan and that he could keep her in line.

The amount of pleasure she was about to experience was necessary and as much a part of her submission as was counting out the number of times he spanked her. Logan stroked harder and faster, finally settling his thumb on the puckered entrance to her back passage and pressing down. As he did so, her orgasm claimed her, and she cried out in ecstasy, her pussy spasming around his finger and her need for him coating his hand.

"Fucking A," breathed Nash as she fell limp over Logan's lap.

"It won't happen again, will it, baby?"

"No, Sir. I'm so sorry."

"I believe you, and so does everybody else."

"Absolutely." Mason rested his hand on her head. "You took your discipline very well. Logan should be proud of you."

"I am," said Logan, the sound of that pride evident in his voice.

"Well done," Zak agreed.

"Indeed," concurred Flynn, who'd wandered over from the other side of the salon.

"That's a damn fine woman you've got there, Logan. I'd better never find out you're not treating her right," grumbled Nash. "Damn fine."

Logan helped her to stand, keeping his hand on her to keep her steady before lifting her into his arms. Cradling her against his chest, he headed back to their stateroom.

∽

Green

"She did what?" Green snarled into the phone.

He wanted to reach through the damn thing and rip Zander Effron's throat out. This should have been so simple. They'd discredit that interfering environmentalist's reputation, fire her and blame the spill, as well as the rising toxicity in the water, on her. Any idiot should have been able to do it. Apparently, not just any idiot. It had been beyond Effron's ability.

"I didn't anticipate HR being so slow to respond to the message I sent them," Effron tried to explain.

"She'd been filing daily reports but hadn't done the one for yesterday. She filed it this morning and downloaded all the files related to this spill for her own records. But that's not the worst of it…"

"You mean it gets better, and your incompetence gets worse?"

Choosing to ignore Eli's insult, the beleaguered CEO continued. "She sent a memo to the Board of Directors and to her HR file, which is how I found out about it. There's this cute little piece of tail that works in HR. She makes sure I know about anything that casts my leadership in a poor light. She thinks letting me screw her whenever I want means she can sleep her way to the top. That's so stupid. How can some women believe you would trust them with anything sensitive or important if you give it up that easily?"

"I don't give a fuck how you get your rocks off." Green was losing patience. "What's in the memo?"

"Right. Well, she basically said I was a fuck up and your stooge. She called into question our business dealings and classified them as a conflict of interest."

So, the pert little hard body had figured that out, had she? Green knew she was screwing one of the team members. He wondered idly if the trained SEAL had taken her ass. Maybe before he killed her, he'd take it. Or better yet, depending on which member it was, he'd make the asshole watch while he did it. Or perhaps make all of them watch to show them what would happen to any of their little fuck toys if they didn't fall into line.

Green's cock began to stiffen. Yeah, that idea had a lot of merit. He stroked his hardening erection. He'd need Paulo to find him a woman to use while he figured out how to make all of this work to his advantage. The idea of taking the little bubble-butted do-gooder's ass was making him hard. Harder still at the idea of doing it with an audience of handcuffed SEALs forced to their knees and made to watch.

Sighing, he considered how best to kill Effron. Effron's death was a foregone conclusion that Green had come to a long time ago. He just needed the little piece of shit's comeuppance to serve the larger goal.

The larger goal being more money and power for Green.

"Don't do anything," Green ordered.

"Anything?" whimpered Effron.

At least he was smart enough to know he'd fucked up royally. "You've done quite enough," answered Green with all the warmth of a shark as it finished feasting on its victim.

CHAPTER 26

Logan

Carrying Dallas into the huge stateroom, Logan closed the door with his foot, throwing her onto the bed.

"You did so well with your punishment." He growled the words, climbing on top of her. "I'm proud of you."

Dallas gazed at him with watery eyes. There was a longing in them that stirred his soul, a recognition that she embraced her submissive side not only to appease their fervor but because it ensured the safety of the entire group. At that moment, he wanted her more than he ever recalled wanting anyone.

"Thank you, Sir."

"And now I have to have you." He brushed his lips over hers, his cock straining to be free. "But the thing is, I'm not in the mood for gentle, and I sense that's what you need."

"No." She reached for him, her fingertips grazing through the stubble at his chin.

"No?"

Lifting from the bed, she kissed his jaw. "I just need you inside me, Sir."

"You're sure?" The shark was hungry for her, ravenous for the kind of carnal contentment only she could bring, but he was conscious that Dallas had just been through an ordeal—her first public spanking. Logan assumed she'd yearn for tenderness from him, reassurance that he cherished her, and he didn't want to do anything that might upset the balance between them. "I don't want to hurt or upset you."

It was an ironic statement from the man who'd happily peppered her ass in front of his friends, but he meant it. He fucking adored spanking Dallas, but punishing her was as much about his worry for her welfare as it was his sexual appetite. He cared as well as craved.

Her lips curled as if she, too, was aware of the irony. "Fuck me now, Sir. Console me later."

Logan chuckled, nuzzling her neck until she moaned. "Is that an order, Ma'am?"

"No, Sir. It was a very respectful request." Her voice was breathy. "That spanking turned me on so much."

"I noticed." Straddling her, he grinned, slowly

unfastening his shirt buttons. "Don't worry, baby. "I'm going to give you what you need." He shrugged out of the garment, discarding it on the floor.

"You're so gorgeous." She licked her lips as she drank in the sight of his muscular torso.

"As are you." He tugged her skirt from her hips, yanking it down until she kicked it away. "I can't get enough of you, Dallas, and I'm going to spend the next hour proving it to you. Off the bed now."

He leapt lithely from the sheets, turning to watch her scramble to her feet. His balls tightened as his gaze took in her reddened backside. He'd marked her as his mate, and now he intended to claim her, possess her body until she was filled with his cum.

"Sir?" Her voice was unsure.

"I want you naked." He motioned to the top she was wearing, his arousal burgeoning as she pulled it over her head, revealing the rest of her wonderful body. "Better. Now, turn around."

The flicker of fear in her eyes was magnificent, but she complied nonetheless, demonstrating her faith in him as she turned her back.

"You're incredible," he praised, moving behind her and curling his arms around her soft skin. "You drive me crazy."

"I feel absurdly vulnerable," she admitted as he nipped at her lobe. Twisting to meet his gaze, she went on, "I'm always naked and exposed, Sir, while you're calm, clothed, and in control."

"That is just the way we both like it," he reminded her as his hands rose to cup the weight of her breasts. Skimming to her nipples, his fingers tweaked and lengthened the buds until she arched against him, her punished ass brushing the bulge in his pants.

"I know," she groaned, her head lolling back against his collar bone.

"But I appreciate your honesty." Logan chuckled as he pinched her sensitive tissue, relishing the gleam of pain in her gaze as it morphed into something needier and more passionate. "Thank you, baby."

"I want you, Sir." She just about managed the words.

"You're gonna have me," he promised. "But first, I'm tying you up."

"You're wh-what?" She turned as much as his arms would permit.

"You heard me, and don't forget how to address me or I'll make sure that ass is so sore you don't sit down for the next week, and then I'll fuck it."

Dallas caught her lower lip between her white teeth, a wonderful bloom of heat developing in her cheeks. "Yes, Sir, but why are you tying me up?"

"Down, actually." He smiled at the puzzlement in her eyes. "I'm going to tie both of your wrists to that bedstead." He gestured to the monstrous bed behind her. "And then fill up your amazing holes."

"A-All of them?" Her eyes widened.

"As many as I like." He cocked his eyebrow at her.

"When I like."

"Oh God."

"Sounds good, huh?" His laugh a deep and resonant sound.

"So good," she confessed as her blush intensified in hue.

"Here." He wandered to the nearby closet, opening the door to reveal various lengths of rope. It wasn't the coarse kind they used at sea but the softer type he liked to bind women with. "Take a look." Strolling back to Dallas, he offered her the rope and waited as she examined it.

"Do all the rooms here have rope in them for binding guests?" she smiled seductively.

"Oh yes." He grinned, watching her long, graceful fingers play with the tethers.

"I've never been bound before, Sir."

He noticed the way her pupils dilated, her nipples still tight buds as their eyes met.

"It won't be anything extreme, I promise." Catching her chin with his thumb and forefinger, he pressed his mouth to hers. "You have to trust me, baby."

"I do, Sir." Her reply was instantaneous. "I trust you."

"Then trust me now." Running his hand through her hair, his fingers caught in her tresses, easing her head back. "Trust me to torment and tantalize, but never to harm you."

Dallas' lips curled up at the corners. "Yes, please."

"Give me your wrists."

Her breathing was ragged as she lifted both hands toward him.

"Good girl." Logan wrapped one length of rope around her left wrist, fastening it into a knot before working on the other wrist. "Turn back toward the bed."

She obeyed, spinning slowly to face the direction he'd ordered, but Logan sensed the nervous energy in her. Dallas' shoulders were tense with apprehension, her chest rising and falling at speed as he took her left hand in his.

"You're beautiful, baby." Lifting her knuckles to his lips, he grazed a caress over them. "So fucking beautiful."

Her lips twitched at the compliment. "Thank you, Sir."

"Stand with your legs apart," he commanded, waiting as she shuffled her feet wider. "Good."

Stretching her hand toward the bedpost, he grabbed the rope and worked it around the wooden structure. The knot wasn't tight, but it would be enough to hold her in place while he devoured her. His cock throbbed impatiently at the blissful idea. Moving to her right side, Logan secured the other rope until she was fettered to both sides of the bedstead.

"There." He smirked, wandering to her rear and

helping himself to her wonderful tits. He'd enjoyed them before, but there was something even sweeter about fondling her now that she could do little to resist. Based on the guttural mewls escaping Dallas' lips, she was inclined to agree. "Now I have you, or I should say, I am *going* to have you."

"Yes, Sir." Her eyes fluttered closed as she wiggled her ass into his swelling erection.

"That's enough of that," he chastised in a playful tone, darting back to swat her tender cheeks.

"Ow, ow, ow!" she yelped.

"Exactly," he growled into her nape as he pulled down his zipper. "I can make it hurt or heavenly baby. Which do you choose?"

"Heaven please, Sir," she whimpered.

"I thought you might say that." He chuckled, releasing his cock. "Lean against the edge of the bed, baby. I already told you that I won't be gentle."

Inching forward, Dallas' breath was thready as she waited for his next move. Relishing her submission, he ran the tip of his cock over her bare ass.

"Your backside is a gorgeous shade."

"Oh God," she moaned.

"And most of my friends have had the pleasure of seeing it."

He couldn't help but tease her, the crimson color of her face now much darker than her tanned behind. Dallas' mortified embarrassment was every bit as arousing as her squirming had been when she'd been hauled over his lap. He couldn't get enough of her sexy little gestures.

"Don't remind me, Sir." She pulled at the ropes. "It was hideous."

"Don't give me that," he chided. "You were horny as hell." Dipping one hand between her outstretched legs, he ran a finger over her labia. After her spanking and orgasm, Dallas was soaking with need. "You still are."

"Someone ignited a fire, Sir." She twisted, her gaze drilling into his face. "Flames I couldn't control."

"Need me to take care of that for you?" Pressing into her, his cock throbbed between her legs, tormenting her with the thing she craved the most.

"Yes, please, Sir."

"Your wish is my command." Tilting her hips back toward him, he found her entrance with ease and pushed into her tight, wet pussy. "Fuck, Dallas."

"Oh God." Thrilled at the sensations and yet unable to properly move, she seemed frantic as he withdrew and slammed into her cunt. "Oh God, yes!"

"You are so fucking good." He filled her over and over, the noises of flesh hitting flesh resounding as their bodies aligned in ecstasy. "Maybe I'll keep you bound to my bed all the time."

"Oh yes." Suspended between his bindings and his body, she had nowhere to go, and as his rhythm intensified, she was pinned to the edge of the bed by the power of his cock.

"You like that?" Holding her at the hip, his free hand rose to her hair, jerking her head back.

"Logan." She hissed his name, her whimper half terrified and half aroused.

"Wrong answer," he snarled, fisting her mane harder until he forced her body into an unyielding arch.

"Sir, please." Her hips rocked, garnering friction from the wood as he took what belonged to him. "Yes, I love it. I love this."

Releasing her hair, his arm snaked around her neck, holding her against him while he hammered into her scintillating body. Again and again, he filled her, trapping her neck in the crook of his arm as he finally detonated.

"Fuuuck." He lurched forward, catching the bedstead to stop himself from collapsing on top of her. "That was magnificent." Pulling back her glorious mane of strawberry blonde hair, he pressed a tender kiss on the side of her neck. Dallas clenched around his semi-erect cock, milking the last of his orgasm from him.

"Thank you, Sir." She sounded reassuringly content as he stretched to meet her lips.

"You're welcome, baby." Straightening, he grabbed her ass, massaging it roughly as he went on. "That was round one, and now I get to decide which hole I enjoy next."

CHAPTER 27

Dallas

Several hours later, Dallas stretched luxuriously in Logan's arms. He'd been ravenous—almost insatiable, but little by little as he'd fucked her repeatedly, sanity had returned to them both.

"You okay?" he purred behind her.

"I don't think I want to sit down any time soon, but a hot shower with a sexy shark shifter ought to fix the rest."

"I can handle that, but I need to talk to you. A conversation I think best had while you're still exhausted and in a very submissive state of mind."

"Logan, whatever is worrying you, let it go. I have something to say to you too. Why not let me go first? It might make whatever you say easier…" She hesitated. "Or incredibly more difficult and terribly awkward."

"Ladies first." He kissed her neck.

"I love you." She blew out a breath. "I know it's way too soon, and I'm not asking you to do or say anything you're not comfortable with…"

Tilting her head back into the crook of his shoulder, he leaned over her, capturing her mouth and silencing her at the same time as his tongue swept through the recesses of her mouth before pulling back.

"I love you too. I think I've known it since that night in the bar. I was afraid if I told you that, you'd run like hell."

"Would that have done me any good?" she teased.

"Nope. I'd have chased you down, slapped your backside silly, and dragged you home. Then I'd have welted your ass before I fucked it… hard."

She giggled, completely unafraid of him but suspecting it wasn't an idle threat. Instead of it making her feel trapped or fearful, she felt safe, loved, and cherished. "Message received, Sir. But did it help?"

Logan expelled his breath with a sigh as he rolled to his back, pulling her close, so her head was on his shoulder, her hand on his chest, and her legs straddling his muscular thigh.

"It did. It was part of what I was going to tell you, but I had decided to tell you the rest first so that when I said it, you'd know what you were getting into."

Dallas sensed he didn't need any response other

than her hugging him close. He might be as alpha a male as she'd ever met, and he certainly qualified as a Dom, but at the end of the day, he was just like any man and needed to know he was loved without any kind of qualification. He made her feel that way, and she wanted him to feel the same.

"Tell me," she urged quietly.

"Okay, you know the really big secret—that we're shark shifters." He paused. "What you don't know is about the Kraken…"

"The mythical sea creature?"

He chuckled. "No, one of two U.S. submarines. The first lies at the bottom of the Sea of Cortez, scuttled there by her five-man crew. The second was a decoy used by the government to cover up that they scuddled the first in order to ensure her secrets never saw the light of day."

"What secrets?"

"That her crew saw the Japanese fleet headed for Pearl Harbor and radioed it in. The War Department didn't warn Pearl, and you know the result. But more than that, it now hides the entrance to a secret base."

"A secret base?" She smiled. "Like in science fiction novels?"

Logan nodded. "Just like. Each member of this unit is descended from the original crew and how we got to be shifters isn't pretty."

"You mean you weren't born this way?"

"No." His jaw clenched.

"But why not use technology—personal submarines, underwater drones, something like that?"

"I think because when it started, this was all they had, and now they see no reason to change. To make a long story short, at a certain age, our families had to give us up, sacrifice us to the Guardian Project. That's where we go at night to patrol the waters and keep the secret of the base and its inhabitants secure."

"People live there?" she gasped. "Why don't they just use submarines or people in SCUBA? Why all the secrecy?"

"Yes, scientists, staff, retired members of the Project, and the like. It's also where we go for medical treatment—regular exams, vaccinations, or if we're hurt or injured."

"Why not just see a regular doctor?"

"Because our bloodwork would set off all kinds of alarms," he explained. "It's not normal. When we're turned into shifters, the gene therapy rewrites our DNA."

"Gene therapy?"

"Yes, how we're transitioned from human to shifter. We've heard they're trying to create more of us, trying to find a better way."

"Define better," she said, frightened for the first time.

"They'll never touch you or any of the others.

They'd have five rogue SEAL/shark-shifters on their hands."

"Five? There are only four of us girls."

"Angel, if you don't know that Nash would lay down his life to keep one or all of you safe, you haven't been paying attention," Logan soothed. "Don't get me wrong, he's a tough sonofabitch, probably the toughest of all, but like the rest of us, he's all in about protecting his family. Any action we took against them wouldn't be pretty and would have major repercussions for all of us. But Devon and some of the rest believe they're trying to breed shark shifters."

"Why?"

"The gene therapy kills more than it transitions."

"That's horrible. Why would your family let them do that to you?"

"Because our families would lose everything and be arrested, tried, and convicted of treason. Either you go along, or they end you."

"Don't you hate your family for that?" she asked.

"No. I understand it, and I was raised knowing I was the most likely to be offered up."

"No wonder you think of your unit as your family."

Logan gave her a reassuring hug. "Yeah, and you and the other girls are a part of that unit. I just wanted you to know everything. If you've changed—oof," he said as she twisted his nipple.

"I may not be the dominant partner in this relationship, but you do *not* get to doubt my commitment to you or those we call family. Got it?"

He chuckled. "Yes, Ma'am. Consider me duly chastised."

There was a knock on the door.

"Come!" Logan called.

Nash stuck his head inside the door. "Dallas, Devon says it's starting. Logan, Devon has arranged a press conference and needs Dallas cleaned up and ready to go in front of the cameras in two hours."

"I don't have anything to wear," Dallas started. "Anything I had was at the hotel."

Nash grinned. "Not to worry, Mason took Shiloh and Trinity, and they got your stuff. They then dragged him into one of those Gucci boutiques and hair places. They'll get you fixed up."

"In other words, we need to get a shower, then I need to leave her in their capable hands."

"Pretty much," Nash replied. "I'd say you have fifteen minutes, twenty at most. Because while Shiloh and Trinity are getting Dallas ready, Devon's going to be prepping you."

"I don't know about this." Dallas tensed. "Cameras?"

"You can do this," said Nash before Logan had a chance to say a word. "You're one of the strongest women I've ever met, and you have an entire familial unit backing you up. Pistris has no idea what's about to happen to them—the term feeding frenzy leaps to mind."

Nash chuckled at his own jest as he left, closing the door behind him while Logan and Dallas rolled their eyes.

"You heard the man," said Logan. "Let's get this party started."

Taking a shower together was something Dallas was beginning to enjoy immensely, even a quick hurried one like this. Logan made sure she felt secure and allowed her to lean against his strength.

As he dried her off, he kissed her shoulder. "We can take a better one later."

"As long as I'm with you, there is nothing better."

He leaned his forehead against hers. "I feel the same way."

Logan looked as if he was about to say more when there was another knock, followed by the sound of Shiloh, Trinity, and Devon entering their stateroom.

"Out," Devon ordered, then realized she'd said it as a command. "Sorry, Logan. We need you to leave so we can prep Dallas for the press conference. Pistris is trying to lay the blame for the spill on Dallas and saying they can't get in touch with her. We need to get out in front of them with our modified version of the truth. I've got friends in the media, so she won't be grilled, but this should go a long way into shutting them down."

"I know when I'm out of my depth," Logan responded, giving her a brief kiss. "I'll be topside and ready to leave with you."

Devon shook her head. "Not the plan." She held up her hand before Logan could growl. "You and the guys are going to set up where you can keep an eye on everything. I've managed to get the one guy with the Mexican government who thinks Pistris is a piece of shit company and is lying through their teeth. He's coming with a detail to take us in. I get to put on my dress uniform and stand up with her. Dallas will be between Ruiz and me. It will show the world that the authorities believe Dallas."

"How'd you get the Mexicans to cooperate?" Logan asked.

"It's in Ruiz's best interest to be seen on the side of cleaning up the oil spill and taking the dirty Americans to task for their carelessness."

"Go on, Logan," said Dallas. "I'll be fine."

"I don't like it, but if Mason is willing to sign off on this plan and Flynn is willing to have you stand with her, then I'll go along. Where will Trin and Shiloh be?"

"Zak is staying here to safeguard them and the yacht and will be our backup if need be," Devon explained. "You guys will already have the other powerboat in a different location for a fast getaway if we need it."

"You girls take care of my lady. I guess I'll go join

the others." He looked Dallas in the eye. "If you don't want to do this, you don't have to. We can take off and keep going. I can keep you safe, and they'll never be able to touch you."

"And have them destroy my reputation, not to mention the environment? Not a chance." She straightened. "If Pistris thinks they can intimidate me and ruin my good name, they'd best think again."

Logan grinned. "We were always an impressive unit on our own. Now that we have you girls? There is nothing that can beat us."

Once he'd gone, Devon turned to Dallas. "He's right. You don't have to do this. Logan is smart, and he can keep you safe. If you want, you can run, and none of us will blame you."

"And let all of you have the fun of bringing these bastards down and protecting our men?" Dallas said cheekily.

"Who said anything about protecting the boys?"

"They want to start breeding super soldiers. I'm a scientist. It doesn't take much to figure out who they want to use for breeding stock, and I don't know about the rest of you, but the only woman Logan is knocking up is me."

Trinity gave her a hug. "I knew you were going to fit in just fine."

Green

Green sat watching the news in his office overlooking the city. The busty blonde kneeling between his legs was giving him an adequate blowjob—good enough to get him off, but not enough to totally distract him. He leaned over and squeezed her ass, which had the added effect of shoving his cock to the back of her throat. Was there anything sweeter than the sound of a woman choking on your dick? Green didn't think so.

"Maybe I should tear your ass up," he snarled, pressing against her anus. "You feel pretty tight back there. Ever taken a man's cock up your ass?"

The girl's fearful look was all it took for him to know that she still had a virginal hole and decide it was just what he needed. He fisted her hair, pulling her off his cock. He loved the sound that it made when it exited her lips, even though she was desperately trying not to lose it.

"Yeah, popping a woman's ass cherry is just what I need."

The blonde softly mewled as he dragged her over to the couch, pulled her to her feet, and bent her over the edge. His cock was damn near to bursting. He probably wouldn't last long, but this was so much better than her less-than-stellar oral skills. She tried to stand up, but Green swatted her ass twice with one hand while pushing her down with the other.

"You gotta know nothing I like better than taking a woman's ass who doesn't want it. Even better is to do it after I've laid a set of pretty stripes across it with my belt."

He felt all the fight go out of her as she slumped over the couch and started to cry. His cock was still wet from her mouth, but the entrance to her ass was tight. Green spat on his hand and rubbed it over her puckered entrance. He didn't care if it hurt her, but it would be easier for him to get the head of his dick inside before slamming it home.

He was just lining up his cock when there was a special news bulletin. Dallas Miles, that interfering eco-freak, was standing alongside that meddlesome JAG lawyer in front of a room full of media.

The lawyer started to talk and give the reporters some background as one of the Mexican officials—who he hadn't been able to bribe—passed out folders with printed information. Fuck. They were so fucked.

"Get out," he snarled at the girl, who didn't even bother to get dressed before running out the door.

"Mr. Green?" said Mawnsey as he stuck his head inside.

"Have our men pick up Driscoll, Effron, Jr., and Admiral Wilson. Separate cars, separate conference rooms. I don't want any of them to know about the others."

"Yes, sir," Mawnsey replied, turning to do Green's

bidding without asking any questions—he liked a man who followed orders without questions.

He probably should have fucked the blonde's ass. Green had a feeling it was going to be a long night.

CHAPTER 28

Green

Stretching, Green climbed off the bed, slowly rolling his neck. The blonde standing beside him might be a little older than his usual type, but she was one hell of a masseuse.

"Will that be all, Mr. Green?" She fluttered her heavily made-up lashes at him.

He drank in her naked body, his cock stirring at her ample breasts. Those would be good to fuck, and God knew he could use the release after the night he'd had.

It had taken hours of terse conversations with Driscoll, Effron Jr., and Wilson to reach any sort of conclusion, and in his gut, Green still wasn't content with the outcome. All three men had committed to helping Green bring down the SEAL unit, who seemed to spawn the women who were now causing so much irritation, but even collectively, Green sensed he'd need more. Mutants like Knight and Lockheart were more than the average man—stronger and more resilient. They were also highly skilled. To end the group entirely, he'd either need the mother of all audacious plans or to pick each man—and their annoying bitches—off, one at a time.

Green didn't much care which way they lurched, so long as, ultimately, the job was done. The guys in white coats at the secret shark base were onto something miraculous, and it was his money that would fund their cutting-edge research. Green didn't want morons like the eco freak and her JAG lawyer muddying his waters. The genetic breeding program was the future—and it had Green's name all over it.

"Sir?" The blonde shifted her weight from one foot to the other, waiting for his verdict.

"Get me a drink." He motioned to the nearby line of decanters. "A large one."

He hadn't made up his mind about her, but she was pretty enough to be useful for an hour while he decided.

"Yes, Sir."

Smiling, she strode away from the impromptu massage, padding over to his glassware. He admired her ass as she walked away. Maybe he'd been wrong to always go for younger women. It seemed this one was not only beautiful but more confident in her own skin.

He turned at the noise of his phone vibrating, reaching for the device and checking the screen. The admiral had sent a new message, and Green's lips curled as he read the lines.

Mr. Green,
I have spoken to the men we discussed.
They're all on board but suggest that
we take the unit out one at a time.
Plans are already in motion for the first.
Wilson

Finally, Wilson was taking this seriously. It was about fucking time.

Hitting reply, Green sank into his leather chair, glancing up to see the blonde pouring his Scotch.

"On your knees," he ordered. "You should always be naked and on your knees when you serve me."

Peering over the expensive glassware, her lips twitched. "Of course, Mr. Green."

She fell gracefully to her knees, concluding the job in hand. Green's brow rose at her dignified obedience, enjoying the way her tits swayed as she shuffled over to replace the decanter.

"Now, bring the drink back here," he instructed. "Slowly."

She smiled, clasping the glass in one hand before she started to crawl. His cock swelled at her compliance, but he forced his attention back to the admiral's message. There would always be a pretty blonde with great tits to entertain him, but the SEAL issue needed handling, and as soon as possible.

Thank you, Admiral.

He typed the reply.

Who and when are we dealing with first?

Wilson responded before the blonde had even completed her tantalizing journey.

Nash Carlton.
Since he's the only one without a
whore in tow, he'll be easy to pick off.

Green grinned at the reply. Despite his frequent misgivings about the admiral, he did like the way the guy's mind worked.

Perfect, he answered as the blonde shuffled to his feet. *How soon can your men set things up?*

"Here you are, Sir." She lowered her gaze as she offered him the Scotch, and reaching for the glass, he admired her full lips and high cheekbones.

Yes, she might be pushing forty, but Green liked her. He would definitely have her stay and satisfy him tonight.

"Polish my dick while I drink."

He gestured to his zipper, easing it down and removing his throbbing cock. If her oral skills were up to scratch, she could take the edge off while he finished up with the admiral.

"Certainly, Mr. Green." Edging between his

thighs, her small fist wrapped around the base of his swelling shaft before her lips enfolded his crown.

"Nice."

He leaned back in his chair, sipping at his drink and watching her for a moment. The vibration of Wilson's reply was almost a distraction, but his concentration flitted to the phone, regardless. Business before pleasure. Green knew the score.

We intercepted some of their communication.
It seems four of them will be away from their yacht—
Carlton included. We intend to exploit this.

That made sense. Their super yacht, *Top Secret*, was damn near impossible to penetrate. It would take Wilson's level of security clearance to even gain access to their personal messages.

So, when?

Green fired off the response just as the blonde's fist disappeared, and she took the full extent of his length deep in her throat.

"Fuck."

He blew out a breath, impressed by her technique. The platinum blonde he'd had there before the latest shitshow blew up had been sadly lacking in this department, but her older counterpart was making it difficult to think.

When the time is right. The admiral replied.
If conditions are conducive, then in
the next twenty-four hours.

Now, this was more like it. Suddenly, he seemed to

have the admiral's full support and an attractive woman who knew how to give head. Things were looking up, after all.

"That's it." Placing his glass on the arm of his chair, his hand slid to her hair, fisting it as she buried his cock deep in her throat again. "Just like that."

As to your other request, Mr. Green,

Wilson's message was definitely an interruption now the blonde was well into her rhythm, but somehow, Green compelled his gaze back to the phone, reading the admiral's latest missives.

The personnel at the base invite
you to meet them on Tuesday.
They're excited to show
you what they're working on.

Yeah, Green bet they were. More likely, they were annoyed that the man paying for their venture had the power to reorganize their week. But that was tough shit. He did have that power.

Letting the phone slip from his fingers, his focus fell to the blonde choking on his cock. Tears were streaming down her face, but she didn't seem to care. Her sole intention seemed to be on pushing Green over the precipice and devouring his cum.

"Hell yeah."

His head rocked back against the leather seat as his climax neared. Wilson could wait. Green would answer him later and confirm the trip to the base.

Hopefully, by then, the notorious Bull Shark known as Nash would already be out of the equation.

∽

Nash

Nash's attention diverted to his phone as it buzzed in his pocket. Watching Mason and Logan deep in conversation about how Devon was helping Dallas, he pulled out the device. Nash's heart rate accelerated at what he found. Sydney Walsh had messaged him! It was no secret that Nash had always had a thing for the ravishing doctor at the secret shark base, but somehow, he'd never found the right moment to tell her how he felt.

Hey Nash,

I've been thinking about you.

Nash's pulse quickened. She'd been thinking about him? Was it possible that she shared his burgeoning feelings?

Can we meet tomorrow?

There's something we need to talk about.

Oh God, she wanted to meet. That was just what Nash wanted to hear! He peered up at the guys, conscious that they might be watching him, but Flynn hadn't returned from his phone call with Devon, and neither Mason nor Logan had glanced his way. Steadying his breath, he sent Sydney an immediate reply.

Hi Sydney,
It's great to hear from you.
I'd love to meet.
Can you get off base?

His imagination ran away with him as he waited for her response. In his mind's eye, he saw them laughing and flirting together over a beer before he took her somewhere more private. Christ, he wanted her so much. The idea of having any time together was intoxicating. Sydney was a great scientist, but her work was so classified, she was rarely permitted to leave the base. This could be the chance he'd been waiting for.

Yes, I'll message you when
and where we can meet.
Looking forward to it!
Sydney x

Nash's brow furrowed at the kiss she'd ended her message with. Much though he longed to believe the sentiment, Sydney had never given him much reason to think they were more than just friends. Still, maybe this was it—her opportunity to let him know she was interested. He certainly hoped so.

"You're quiet, Nash."

Nash's gaze rose at Logan's wry tone.

"Gotta hot date, have you?" Logan teased.

Nash's lips twitched at the accuracy of his friend's jibe. He wouldn't tell the others about his rendezvous with Sydney. He didn't want twenty-four hours full of their constant quips. Hopefully, things would develop with the sexy doctor, then he'd update them.

"Nothing you need to worry about, Logan." He fixed his Mako friend with a stare. "Nothing you need to worry about."

CHAPTER 29

Dallas

The only thing that kept Dallas from bolting as they walked up to the podium, where Devon introduced her and Ruiz began handing out folders with the documents and correspondence they'd downloaded, was knowing Logan, Flynn, Mason, and Nash were secreted up in the rafters with high-powered rifles. It didn't hurt that she also knew *Top Secret* was standing by with Zak and the other girls. They'd hidden one of the yacht's power boats so that if things went to rat shit, they could get the hell out of there.

Both she and Devon were wearing two-way communication devices in their ears, and there were times it was hard not to laugh.

"Damn, little girl," crooned Flynn over the link, "your ass looks spectacular in those dress whites."

"Cut the chatter," ground out Mason.

"Well, it does." Flynn chuckled. "Come on, you have to admit that ass in that white skirt looks amazing. I think we should all get dress whites for the girls that include white corsets, tight white micro-minis, and Navy headgear… nothing else. We could have all kinds of fun."

"You're a sick bastard," Nash growled.

"You ladies will take note that the only one not agreeing with Flynn is the guy who isn't getting laid on a regular basis," laughed Logan.

"Just ignore them," whispered Devon to Dallas. "Sometimes they're like little boys with a new toy."

"Best fuck toy ever," quipped Flynn, making Devon smile.

Devon stepped up to the podium and began. For the next two hours, Devon, Ruiz, and Dallas presented their case to the public about the Pistris spill. Devon had chosen wisely. For the most part, the news media and networks who'd been invited were friendly and sympathetic to their cause.

There had been an audible gasp when the reporters began to look at the irrefutable evidence that not only did Dallas not have any culpability, but that she had been doing everything in her power to stop the spill, mitigate the damage, and find out who was responsible.

"Here it comes," whispered Flynn, all traces of

amusement gone from his voice as he watched Devon speak.

"It is our belief that there is a larger threat to the environment than just the spill itself. The recent analysis of the water surrounding the rig shows carcinogens and toxic waste that would not have come from the rig. You will note that part of what we were able to uncover would indicate that the current leadership at Pistris was involved in some less than ethical dealings with both a major shareholder and a local businessman…"

Devon continued to lead, and Dallas admired her calm and cool demeanor. She also loved the way Flynn spoke to her as if no one else could hear, reassuring her, telling her how proud he was of her, and helping relieve the tension from how very much he wanted to ruck that skirt up around her hips and shove his dick up inside her. Dallas almost spat her water when he said that and was floored that Devon's only response was a slight upturn of the corners of her mouth.

"I have Dallas Miles, who used to work for Pistris and who they are trying to blame for the spill, here to answer your questions." Devon glanced in Dallas' direction.

"Commander Bradford, can you tell us why you and Captain Ruiz are here today?" asked one reporter. "Is Ms. Miles your client?"

"In the spirit of full disclosure, Dallas is a friend of mine. When she came to me with what she had, I agreed with her scientific assessment of the situation. I felt it was imperative we share what we knew to be true with the Mexican authorities as it is their water and environment that Pistris is polluting. Captain Ruiz examined our evidence and came to the same conclusion. He suggested we alert the media as it appeared Pistris, in trying to cover its shoddy maintenance and perhaps criminal activities, planned to blame Dallas, who had been reporting her findings all along."

"As for being my client, no. I am a JAG attorney, and I work for the United States Government." Devon's back straightened. "The Judge Advocate General, to be precise. I am here in Mexico on leave and was asked to arrange for Admiral Warrenton's body to be sent home for interment in Arlington. When Dallas realized what Pistris was up to, she asked for my advice *as a friend.*"

"You tell 'em, little girl," Flynn purred.

"Yes," Captain Ruiz agreed, stepping up to the microphone. "When Commander Bradford and Ms. Miles showed me what they had, I thanked them for bringing it to our attention. We will be asking the CEO of Pistris, the as-yet unnamed board member, and the man we believe to be their local contact to come in for questioning. My government is most concerned about what is being done to our fragile ecosystem and will demand reparations to include cleanup and monetary damages."

The reporters wanted to ask Dallas questions, and from the moment she stepped up to the podium to begin answering them, her ear was full of Logan's voice as he kept her centered on the job at hand and reassured her that the situation was under control.

At the two-hour mark, Devon stepped back up to the microphone and brought the press conference to an end. Captain Ruiz offered to stay behind to answer additional questions and said he would field any and all requests for interviews with Dallas.

They were barely out of sight of the media and their cameras when Flynn and Logan were beside them, leading them, along with Mason and Nash, out to the boat. They hopped in, untied, and headed back for *Top Secret*.

"Now what?" Dallas blew out a breath, relieved.

"We go back to *Top Secret*, get underway, and go lie low for a few days," Logan told her. "The team can keep an eye on what's going on not only with the media but at the rig. Being a shark-shifter gives us a big advantage in doing any kind of surveillance work at sea."

"How do you think we did?" she asked Devon.

"I think we hit just the right note. Ruiz is going to be pleased. This will do a lot for his career and will go a long way in improving Mexico's reputation in the environmental community. I don't think they're going to be able to touch you. If I was Barney from the rig or Barry Driscoll of Oceanic Adventures, I'd be very worried. There's no way guys like Green or Effron take the blame for this kind of shit."

"What'll happen to Driscoll's company?" asked Nash.

"Devon did some digging. It seems Green was a silent partner in the business," Flynn replied. "I think Trinity is going to be looking for a new job."

"That's not news. There's no way Zak was letting her go back to work for that sleazebag," Nash chuckled.

"Yeah, but Devon got to thinking if we can force Green out, we might be able to pick up that company and let the girls run it. Think of it—two top SCUBA divers, two shark experts, and Shiloh used to be a professor. Between Shiloh, Trin, and Dallas, they could take that company and do something special." Flynn smiled.

"Dallas, no one is trying to speak for you…," Devon reassured.

"Fuck that," Logan countered. "I sure as hell am. This would give her a job that wasn't out on a rig doing something where she could educate people about fossil fuels and the environment."

Dallas all but wiggled like a happy Labrador puppy. "Oh, I love that idea. No more running around the world, and doing something I could feel good about? I am so in. And if we can't buy Driscoll's company, I have a lot of money invested in savings and retirement plans."

Mason nodded. "So does Shiloh, who said the same thing. She even thinks there's a possibility of doing something in conjunction with the university at Coronado or with one of the shark studies."

Devon smiled. "Sometimes, you guys are about as subtle as a group of freight trains. In other words, Dallas, they can keep you close. I'm just waiting for the Oceanic Whitetip here to figure out how and why I should leave my career with JAG." Before Flynn could respond to her veiled accusation, she took his face in her hands and kissed him deeply as she leaned into his body. "And I have all the reason I need to do it staring back at me."

Flynn's arms slid around her, his hands falling on her ass. "I love you, little girl."

"I love you too, Master," she purred.

"Okay, you two, neutral corners until we get back to *Top Secret*," snarled Nash.

By the time they joined up with the yacht, Shiloh was waiting for them.

"Zak says we're ready to get underway as soon as we have the boat tied up and Trinity has food. And if you're wondering, my job is to look pretty," she laughed.

"No, Shi, your job is to keep Mason so well laid, he stays on an even keel, and the rest of us don't have to deal with what a moody bastard he can be," Flynn laughed as he helped Devon and Dallas onto *Top Secret*. "By the way, I wasn't kidding about those new uniforms."

They all mirrored his laughter.

"Of course, you weren't." Mason smirked. "Did you behave yourself?"

"Why do you always ask me that?" asked Shiloh.

"Because of all the girls that are a part of this unit, you're the one with the worst track record for doing as you're told," Mason answered, drawing her into his arms and walking her backward as he kissed her thoroughly.

"Anyone want to bet that the Great White means to school the professor in all the ways he can fuck her stupid?" Flynn leered.

"I'll grant you, the boss means to get inside her, but fucking a woman as smart as Shiloh stupid would take more fucking than even the Great White could pull off," Nash sneered.

"I'd say about the same amount as a certain scientist at the shark city," quipped Flynn.

"Yeah," teased Logan, "must be that whole doctor thing."

Nash grumbled under his breath and stalked off toward the conference room that often doubled as the communal dining space. "I'm going to get some chow."

"You two are awful," scolded Devon.

"I take it there's a doctor in the shark city?" asked Dallas.

"Yeah, Dr. Sydney Walsh, she's their chief research scientist, but I don't think she knows about the experiments and their planned breeding program," Logan explained.

The two couples headed up to join their compatriots, their brothers-in-arms, who had become a family and managed to incorporate the women with whom they were involved. Dallas had only been with them a few days but already felt closer to them than she had her birth family. And Logan? She was stupid in love with Logan and was so glad they didn't have to live some kind of fantasy life behind closed doors. They could live it out in the open amongst their friends with nothing to hide.

"You did great, baby. I was so proud of you," he said, wrapping his arm around her. "And you're okay with the idea of throwing in with the other girls?"

Dallas laughed. "Let's see, I get three best girlfriends, a bunch of protective older brothers, and a sexy shark shifter who can see to all of my needs and not think I'm weird. Yeah, I'm okay with that. I love you, Logan."

"I love you too." He nuzzled her. "Let's go get you something to eat."

"Aren't you hungry?"

"Ravenous. Only Trinity hasn't figured out how to serve pussy at the table yet."

Nash

He couldn't remember a time he'd ever been happier or more at peace. They weren't clear yet of the Admiral's death, but they were working on it. He had faith in his team and the women that had chosen to commit their lives to them.

EPILOGUE

A secret military base beneath the waters of the Sea of Cortez didn't have many amenities. Luckily for those who had created the base, those who lived and worked there had been convinced that the base and its residents were there for a higher purpose—a higher call to duty. Once upon a time, Dr. Sydney Walsh had believed that. That time had long passed.

It wasn't that the base's designers hadn't tried—there were different places and types of recreation, a state-of-the-art medical facility as well as different places to eat and drink. Officers at the rank of Commander or above could put in for quarters that were more spacious and better appointed. Some even had a private bath. The thing they couldn't do was see or smell the ocean or sky. They were trapped beneath the water, beneath a scuttled submarine, and it often felt like they lived in a coffin. There was no unmonitored communication and only those without close ties to those outside the Guardian Project were *encouraged* to apply.

Sydney snorted. Encouraged was a nice way to put it. Coerced was more like it.

Sitting cross-legged on her bed, she stared down at the lab results. Lab results she never should have had from bloodwork, tissue samples and genetic material she never should have had. Her curiosity about the those who protected both the Kraken and the base had always been at the back of her mind, but as she got to know the men, it increased exponentially, especially where Captain Nash Carlton was concerned.

Sydney was no geneticist, but she was a research scientist and was pretty damn sure she knew what these tests were showing… and it was monstrous.

Recruited by Admiral Warrenton to come on as one of the researchers right out of M.I.T. The offer had been too lucrative to turn her back on and walk away. In exchange for forgiveness of all her student loans and a highly competitive salary and benefits package, Sydney has signed on for a ten-year exclusive and highly confidential assignment. Thus, had begun her tenure at the secret base beneath the waves. Officially known as El Jardin Secreto, the residents affectionately called it "Shark City."

On a number of occasions, she'd been asked to perform blood tests and do an analysis of the test results for the team that protected the Guardian Project. The five men—Mason Lockhart, Zak Vance, Flynn Michaels, Logan Knight and Nash Carlton—had been given the miraculous ability to shift from human to shark and back again.

These guys were no cartoon characters from Japanese Anime or the comic books. They weren't some kind of were-shark with a grotesque form—they were either human or shark and nothing in between. When in their shark form, they were indistinguishable from their non-shifting brethren with two notable exceptions: they were bigger and more powerful, and they retained their ability to think like a human.

Originally, she had thought of them as freaks, then as a necessary evil to keep the secrets of the Kraken and the hidden base. But as she'd gotten to know them, she'd learned they had distinct personalities and all of them had an underlying sadness that was tied to their mutation and their duty. They had been told their obligation to the Kraken was all that mattered, and they believed that until Mason had fallen hard for Shiloh Whittaker.

Mason and Shiloh both believed that the deaths of Shiloh's parents were tied somehow to the Kraken. Zak's girl, Trinity, had been at the party where the Admiral was killed. Devon, Flynn's woman was a JAG lawyer. The newest of the lot was Dallas Miles, an environmentalist who had stolen Logan's heart. All four men were so much happier and at peace, but

Sydney sensed a growing discontent. She knew it was her duty to report it, but she'd grown fond of the SEAL unit that protected the hidden base and wanted to see them happy.

The only one who didn't seem to even want a meaningful relationship with a woman was Nash Carlton, the Bull Shark. There had been a time he had been a frequent visitor to the base's brothel, but for the past few months he only showed up at the base to eat or if he was ordered to report.

When she'd begun, Sydney had believed in the program and the work they did. Without having to answer to anyone or being subjected to any oversight groups, they had been able to make amazing strides in medical science. But if what she was looking at was what she feared it was, someone was perverting their research. They had to be stopped—at any cost.

Thank you for reading Wicked Predator. The next book in the Masters of the Deep series is Deadly Predator.

Dangerous, Daunting and Deadly.

. . .

Nash Carlton is a Bull of a man, A strong and silent protector, In an ocean of gliding monsters. Eli Green is a snake determined to strike, A man resolved to destroy Nash's SEAL unit, one shifter at a time.

But when the woman Nash desires Becomes Green's latest target, He has no choice but to unleash the animal inside.

It's time Green was annihilated.

1-Click Deadly Predator today!

ABOUT FELICITY BRANDON

Felicity Brandon is a USA Today bestselling author. She loves the darker side of romance, and writes sexy, suspenseful stories, with strong themes of bondage and submission. You'll find her either at her laptop, at the gym, or rocking out to her favourite music.

Sign up for FREE sexy reads here! https://felicitybrandonwrites.com/newsletter/

Amazon sales page: http://author.to/FelicityBrandon

Website: https://felicitybrandonauthor.com/

Social media links: Facebook: https://www.facebook.com/felicity.brandon.3

Author page: https://www.facebook.com/FelicityBrandonRomance/

Reader group: https://www.facebook.com/groups/FierceAF/

BookBub: https://www.bookbub.com/authors/felicity-brandon

Goodreads: https://www.goodreads.com/author/show/6892310.felicitybrandon

ALSO BY FELICITY BRANDON

Ensnared Desire

Hyland's Property

Chased

Her Dark Protector

ABOUT DELTA JAMES

Other books by Delta James: https://www.deltajames.com/

As a USA Today bestselling romance author, Delta James aims to captivate readers with stories about complex heroines and the dominant alpha males who adore them. For Delta, romance is more than just a love story; it's a journey with challenges and thrills along the way.

After creating a second chapter for herself that was dramatically different than the first, Delta now resides in Virginia where she relaxes on warm summer evenings with her lovable pack of basset hounds as they watch the birds of prey soaring overhead and the fireflies dancing in the fading light. When not crafting fast-paced tales, she enjoys horseback riding, hiking, and white-water rafting.

Her readers mean the world to her, and Delta tries to interact personally to as many messages as she can. If you'd like to chat or discuss books, you can find Delta on Instagram, Facebook, and in her private reader group https://www.facebook.com/groups/348982795738444.

If you're looking for your next bingeable series, you can get a FREE story by joining her newsletter https://www.subscribepage.com/VIPlist22019.

ALSO BY DELTA JAMES

Syndicate Masters: Northern Lights

Alliance

Complication

Judgement

Syndicate Masters

The Bargain

The Pact

The Agreement

The Understanding

Masters of Valor

Prophecy

Illusion

Deception

Inheritance

Masters of the Savoy

Advance

Negotiation

Submission

Contract

Bound

Release

Fated Legacy

Touch of Fate

Touch of Darkness

Touch of Light

Touch of Fire

Touch of Ice

Touch of Destiny

Masters of the Deep

Silent Predator

Fierce Predator

Savage Predator

Wicked Predator

Deadly Predator

Ghost Cat Canyon

Determined

Untamed

Bold

Fearless

Strong

Boxset

Tangled Vines

Corked

Uncorked

Decanted

Breathe

Full Bodied

Late Harvest

Boxset 1

Boxset 2

Mulled Wine

Wild Mustang

Hampton

Mac

Croft

Noah

Thom

Reid

Box Set #1

Box Set #2

Wayward Mates

In Vino Veritas

Brought to Heel

Marked and Mated

Mastering His Mate

Taking His Mate

Claimed and Mated

Claimed and Mastered

Hunted and Claimed

Captured and Claimed

Printed in Great Britain
by Amazon